# ROBINSON CRUSOE

DANIEL DEFOE (*c.* 1660–1731), one of the most famous writers in English literature, was born in London, the son of James Foe, a butcher. It was Daniel who changed his name to De Foe or Defoe in about 1705.

Politics occupied quite a bit of Defoe's earlier life. He was an opponent of King James II, and had supported the Duke of Monmouth in his short-lived uprising in 1685. When the Glorious Revolution of 1688 was successful, and William III was on the throne, Defoe became one of his personal friends.

This led to his becoming employed, after failing miserably as a businessman, as a writer for the Government. At the same time, however, he pursued an independent line as a writer of pamphlets – often satirical – on various social issues. Although this landed him in prison in 1702, he was soon reinstated, and in 1706 formed part of the team sent to Scotland to negotiate the terms of union with England.

In 1709, a sailor named Alexander Selkirk was rescued

after having lived alone for three years on a desert island in the Pacific. When Defoe turned to full-time writing, this episode fired his imagination – and the result, in 1719, was the publication of *Robinson Crusoe*. The book has become so famous that it has lent its name to the whole genre of castaway literature, which are called by their French name of *robinsonnades*. Defoe's particular strength is in meticulous detail, giving the reader the impression that he is not reading fiction, but a historical report.

Several other adventure stories followed, including *Moll Flanders* (1722), and other works, of which the most famous is *A Journal of the Plague Year* (also 1722). In all, including pamphlets, Defoe authored over 250 works.

Defoe has often been compared to Jonathan Swift, the author of *Gulliver's Travels*. Swift, however, complained of Defoe's occasional moral tone and seriousness. Puffin agree with Swift, and therefore this abridged edition concentrates on the essential story-line of the book.

*Some other Puffin Classics to enjoy*

THE CORAL ISLAND
R. M. Ballantyne

THE RED BADGE OF COURAGE
Stephen Crane

THE THREE MUSKETEERS
Alexandre Dumas

DANIEL DEFOE

# The Life and Adventures of
# Robinson Crusoe

PUFFIN BOOKS

PUFFIN BOOKS

Published by the Penguin Group
Penguin Books Ltd, 27 Wrights Lane, London W8 5TZ, England
Penguin Putnam Inc., 375 Hudson Street, New York, New York 10014, USA
Penguin Books Australia Ltd, Ringwood, Victoria, Australia
Penguin Books Canada Ltd, 10 Alcorn Avenue, Toronto, Ontario, Canada M4V 3B2
Penguin Books (NZ) Ltd, Private Bag 102902, NSMC, Auckland, New Zealand

Penguin Books Ltd, Registered Offices: Harmondsworth, Middlesex, England

First published 1719
Published in Puffin Books 1986
Reissued in this edition 1994
20

This abridgement, by Robin Waterfield,
copyright © Puffin Books, 1986
All rights reserved

Filmset by Datix International Limited, Bungay, Suffolk
Printed in England by Clays Ltd, St Ives plc
Set in 12/15 pt Monophoto Plantin

I was born in the year 1632 in the city of York, of a good family, though not of that country, my father being a foreigner of Bremen who settled first at Hull. He got a good estate by merchandise, and leaving off his trade lived afterward at York, from whence he had married my mother, whose relations were named Robinson, a very good family in that country, and from whom I was called Robinson Kreutznaer; but by the usual corruption of words in England, we are now called, nay, we call ourselves and write our name, Crusoe, and so my companions always called me.

Being the third son of the family and not bred to any trade, my head began to be filled very early with rambling thoughts. I would be satisfied with nothing but going to sea, and my inclination to this led me so strongly against the will, nay, the commands of my father, and against all the entreaties and persuasions of my mother and other friends, that there seemed to be something fatal in that propension of nature tending directly to the life of misery which was to befall me.

My father, a wise and grave man, gave me

serious and excellent counsel against what he foresaw was my design. He called me one morning
into his chamber, and expostulated very warmly
with me upon this subject. He asked me what
reasons more than a mere wandering inclination I
had for leaving my father's house and my native
country, where I had a prospect of raising my
fortune by application and industry. He told me it
was men of desperate fortunes on the one hand, or
of aspiring, superior fortune on the other, who
went abroad upon adventures; that these things
were all either too far above me, or too far below
me; that mine was the middle state, which he had
found by long experience was the best state in the
world. He bid me observe it, and I should always
find, that the calamities of life were shared among
the upper and lower part of mankind; but that the
middle station had the fewest disasters, and was
not exposed to so many vicissitudes as the higher
or lower part of mankind.

After this, he pressed me earnestly, and in the
most affectionate manner, not to play the young
man, not to precipitate myself into miseries which
nature and the station of life I was born in seemed
to have provided against; that I was under no
necessity of seeking my bread; that he would do
well for me and endeavour to enter me fairly into
the station of life which he had been just recom-
mending to me; and that if I was not very easy
and happy in the world, it could only be my own
fate or fault that must hinder it, and that he

should have nothing to answer for, having thus discharged his duty in warning me against measures which he knew would be to my hurt: in a word, that as he would do very kind things for me if I would stay and settle at home as he directed, so he would not have so much hand in my misfortunes as to give me any encouragement to go away; and though he said he would not cease to pray for me, yet he would venture to say to me, that if I did take this foolish step, God would not bless me, and I would have leisure hereafter to reflect upon having neglected his counsel when there might be none to assist in my recovery.

I was sincerely affected with this discourse, and I resolved not to think of going abroad any more, but to settle at home according to my father's desire. But alas! A few days wore it all off; and in short, to prevent any more of my father's importunities, in a few weeks after, I resolved to run quite away from him.

It was not till almost a year after this that I broke loose, though in the meantime I continued obstinately deaf to all proposals of settling to business, and frequently expostulating with my father and mother, about their being so positively determined against what they knew my inclinations prompted me to. But being one day at Hull, where I went casually, and without any purpose of making an elopement that time; but I say, being there, and one of my companions being going by sea to London in his father's ship, and prompting me to go with them, I consulted neither father or mother any more, nor so much as sent them word of it; but leaving them to hear of it as they might, without asking God's blessing, or my father's, without any consideration of circumstances or consequences, and in an ill hour, God knows, on the first of September 1651 I went on board a ship bound for London. Never any young adventurer's misfortunes, I believe, began sooner, or continued longer, than mine. The ship was no sooner gotten out of the Humber, but the wind began to blow and the waves to rise in a most frightful manner; and as I had never been at sea before, I was most inexpressibly sick in body and terrified in my mind. I began now seriously to reflect upon what I had done, and how justly I was overtaken by the judgement of Heaven for my wicked leaving my father's house, and abandoning my duty; all the good counsel of my parents, my father's tears and my mother's entreaties, came now fresh into my mind; and my conscience reproached me with the contempt of advice, and the breach of my duty to God and my father.

All this while the storm increased, and the sea, which I had never been upon before, went very high, though nothing like what I have seen many times since; no, nor like what I saw a few days after: but it was enough to affect me then, who was but a young sailor, and had never known anything of the matter. I expected every wave would have swallowed us up, and that every time the ship fell down, as I thought, in the trough or hollow of the sea, we should never rise more; and in this agony of mind I made many vows and resolutions, that if it would please God here to spare my life this one voyage, if ever I got my foot upon dry land again, I would go directly home to my father, and never set it into a ship again while I lived; that I would take this advice, and never run myself into such miseries as these any more. Now I saw plainly the goodness of his observations about the middle station of life, how easy, how comfortably he had lived all his days, and never had been exposed to tempests at sea or troubles on shore; and I resolved that I would, like a true repenting prodigal, go home to my father.

These wise and sober thoughts continued all the while the storm continued, and indeed some time after; but the next day the wind was abated and the sea calmer; towards night the weather cleared up, the wind was quite over, and a charming fine evening followed; the sun went down perfectly clear and rose so the next morning; and having little or no wind and a smooth sea, the sun shining upon it, the sight was, as I thought, the most delightful that ever I saw.

I had slept well in the night, and was now no more seasick but very cheerful, looking with wonder upon the sea that was so rough and terrible the day before, and could be so calm and so pleasant in so little time after. And now, lest my good resolutions should continue, my companion, who had indeed enticed me away, comes to me. 'Well, Bob,' says he, clapping me on the shoulder, 'how do you do after it? I warrant you were frightened, weren't you, last night, when it blew but a cap full of wind?' 'A cap full d' you call it?' said I, ' 'twas a terrible storm.' 'A storm, you fool, you,' replies he, 'do you call that a storm? Why, it was nothing at all; give us but a good ship and sea room, and we think nothing of such a squall of wind as that; but you're but a freshwater sailor, Bob; come, let us make a bowl of punch and we'll forget all that; d' ye see what charming weather 'tis now?' To make short this sad part of my story, we went the old way of all sailors, the punch was made, and I was made drunk with it, and in that one night's wickedness I drowned all my repentance, and my reflections upon my past conduct, and all my resolutions for my future.

The sixth day of our being at sea we came into Yarmouth bay; the wind having been contrary and the weather calm, we had made but little way since the storm. Here we were obliged to come to anchor, and here we lay, the wind continuing contrary, for seven or eight days. On the eighth day it blew a terrible storm indeed, and now I began to see terror and amazement in the faces even of the seamen themselves. The master, though vigilant to the business of preserving the ship, yet as he went in and out of his cabin by me, I could hear him softly to himself say several times, 'Lord, be merciful to us, we shall be all lost, we shall be all undone'; and the like.

I was dreadfully frightened. I got up out of my cabin, and looked out; but such a dismal sight I had never seen: the sea went mountains high, and broke upon us every three or four minutes; when I could look about, I could see nothing but distress round us. Two ships that lay near us we found had cut their masts by the board, being deep laden; and our men cried out that a ship which lay about a mile ahead of us was foundered. Two more ships, being driven from their anchors, were run out to sea, and that with not a mast standing. The light ships fared the best, as not so much labouring in the sea.

Anyone may judge what a condition I must be in at all this, who was but a young sailor, and who had been in such a fright before at but a little. But the worst was not come yet; the storm continued with such fury, that the seamen themselves acknowledged they had never known a worse. We had a good ship, but she was deep laden, and wallowed in the sea, so that the seamen every now and then cried out she would founder. It was my advantage in one respect, that I did not know what they meant by 'founder' till I inquired. However, the storm was so violent, that I saw what is not often seen: the master, the boatswain, and some others more sensible than the rest, at their prayers, and expecting every moment that the ship would go to the bottom. In the middle of the night, and under all the rest of our distresses, one of the men that had been down on purpose to see, cried out we had sprung a leak; another said there was four foot of water in the hold. Then all hands were called to the pump. At that very word my heart, as I thought, died within me, and I fell backwards upon the side of my bed where I sat, into the cabin. However, the men roused me, and told me that I that was able to do nothing before, was as well able to pump as another; at which I stirred up and went to the pump, and worked very heartily. While this was doing, the master, seeing some light colliers, who not able to ride out the storm, were obliged to slip and run away to sea and would come near us, ordered to fire a gun as a signal of distress. I, who knew nothing what that meant, was so surprised that I thought the ship had broke, or some dreadful thing had happened.

We worked on, but the water increasing in the hold, it was apparent that the ship would founder, and though the storm began to abate a little, yet as it was not possible she could swim till we might run into a port, so the master continued firing guns for help; and a light ship just ahead of us ventured a boat out to help us. It was with the utmost hazard the boat came near us, but it was impossible for us to get on board, or for the boat to lie near the ship's side, till at last, the men rowing very heartily and venturing their lives to save ours, our men cast them a rope over the stern with a buoy to it, which they after great labour and hazard took hold of, and we hauled them close under our stern and got all into their boat. It was to no purpose for them or us after we were in the boat to think of reaching their own ship, so all agreed to let her drive and only to pull her in towards shore as much as we could, and our master promised them that if the boat was staved upon shore he would make it good to their master; so partly rowing and partly driving, our boat bent away to the norward, sloping towards the shore almost as far as Winterton Ness.

We were not much more than a quarter of an hour out of our ship but we saw her sink, and then I understood for the first time what was meant by a ship foundering in the sea.

While we were in this condition, the men yet labouring at the oars to bring the boat near the shore, we could see, when, our boat mounting the waves, we were able to see the shore, a great many people running to assist us when we should come near, but we made but slow progress nor were we able to reach the shore, till being past the light-house at Winterton, the shore falls off to the westward towards Cromer, and so the land broke off a little the violence of the wind. Here we got in, and, though not without much difficulty, got all safe on shore, and walked afterwards on foot to Yarmouth, where, as unfortunate men, we were used with great humanity as well by the magistrates of the town, who assigned us good quarters, as by particular merchants and owners of ships, and had money given us sufficient to carry us either to London or back to Hull, as we thought fit.

Had I now had the sense to have gone back to Hull, and have gone home, I had been happy, and my father, an emblem of our Blessed Saviour's parable, had even killed the fatted calf for me; for hearing the ship I went away in was cast away in Yarmouth, it was a great while before he had any assurance that I was not drowned.

## 2

My comrade, who had helped to harden me
before, and who was the master's son, was now
less forward than I; the first time he spoke to me
after we were at Yarmouth, which was not till two
or three days, for we were separated in the town
to several quarters; I say, the first time he saw me,
it appeared his tone was altered, and looking very
melancholy and shaking his head, asked me how I
did, and telling his father who I was, and how I
had come this voyage only for a trial in order to
go farther abroad; his father turning to me with a
very grave and concerned tone, 'Young man,' says
he, 'you ought never to go to sea any more, you
ought to take this for a plain and visible token that
you are not to be a seafaring man.' 'Why, sir,' said
I, 'will you go to sea no more?' 'That is another
case,' said he. 'It is my calling, and therefore my
duty; but as you made this voyage for a trial, you
see what a taste Heaven has given you of what you
are to expect if you persist; perhaps this is all
befallen us on your account, like Jonah in the ship
of Tarshish. Pray,' continues he, 'what are you?
And on what account did you go to sea?' Upon

that I told him some of my story; at the end of which he burst out with a strange kind of passion. 'What had I done,' says he, 'that such an unhappy wretch should come into my ship? I would not set my foot in the same ship with thee again for a thousand pounds.'

We parted soon after, for I made him little answer, and I saw him no more; which way he went, I know not. As for me, having some money in my pocket, I travelled to London by land; and there, as well as on the road, had many struggles with myself, as to what course of life I should take, and whether I should go home or go to sea.

As to going home, shame opposed my best impulses; and it immediately occurred to me how I should be laughed at among the neighbours, and should be ashamed to see, not my father and mother only, but even everybody else.

I have since often observed how young people are not ashamed to sin, and yet are ashamed to repent; not ashamed of the action for which they ought justly to be esteemed fools, but are ashamed of the returning, which only can make them be esteemed wise men.

In this state of life, however, I remained some time, uncertain what measures to take, and what course of life to lead. An irresistible reluctance continued to going home; and as I stayed awhile, the remembrance of the distress I had been in wore off; and as that abated, the little inclination I had in my desires to a return wore off with it, till at last I quite laid aside the thoughts of it, and looked out for a voyage.

It was my lot to fall into pretty good company in London, which does not always happen to such loose and unguided young fellows as I then was; the devil generally not omitting to lay some snare for them very early; but it was not so with me. I first fell acquainted with the master of a ship who had been on the coast of Guinea, and who, having had very good success there, was resolved to go again; and who, taking a fancy to my conversation, which was not at all disagreeable at that time, hearing me say I had a mind to see the world, told me if I would go the voyage with him I should be at no expense; I should be his messmate and his companion, and if I could carry anything with me, I should have all the advantage of it that the trade would admit; and perhaps I might meet with some encouragement.

I embraced the offer, and entering into a strict friendship with this captain, who was an honest and plain-dealing man, I went the voyage with him, and carried a small investment with me, which by the disinterested honesty of my friend the captain I increased very considerably; for I carried about £40 in such toys and trifles as the captain directed me to buy. This £40 I had mustered together by the assistance of some of my relations whom I corresponded with, and who, I believe, got my father, or at least my mother, to contribute so much as that to my first adventure.

This was the only voyage which I may say was successful in all my adventures, and which I owe to the integrity and honesty of my friend the captain, under whom also I got a competent knowledge of the mathematics and the rules of navigation, learned how to keep an account of the ship's course, take an observation, and in short, to understand some things that were needful to be understood by a sailor: for, as he took delight to introduce me, I took delight to learn; and, in a word, this voyage made me both a sailor and a merchant; for I brought home 5 pounds, 9 ounces of gold dust, which yielded me in London at my return almost £300, and this filled me with those aspiring thoughts which have since so completed my ruin.

I was now set up for a Guinea trader; and my friend, to my great misfortune, dying soon after his arrival, I resolved to go the same voyage again, and I embarked in the same vessel with one who was his mate in the former voyage, and had now got the command of the ship. This was the unhappiest voyage that ever man made; for though I did not carry quite £100 of my new gained wealth, so that I had £200 left, which I lodged with my friend's widow, who was very just to me, yet I fell into terrible misfortunes in this voyage. Our ship making her course towards the Canary Islands, or rather between those islands and the African shore, was surprised in the grey of the morning by a Turkish rover of Sallee, who gave chase to us with all the sail she could make. We crowded also as much canvas as our yards would spread, or our masts carry, to have got clear; but finding the pirate gained upon us and would certainly come up with us in a few hours, we prepared to fight; our ship having twelve guns, and the rogue eighteen. About three in the afternoon he came up with us, and bringing to by mistake, just athwart our quarter, instead of athwart our stern, as he intended, we brought eight of our guns to bear on that side, and poured in a broadside upon him, which made him sheer off again, after returning our fire, and pouring in also his small-shot from near two hundred men which he had on board. However, we had not a man touched, all our men keeping close. He prepared to attack us again, and we to defend ourselves; but coming next time upon our other quarter, he entered sixty men upon our decks, who immediately fell to cutting and hacking the decks and rigging. We plied them with small-shot, half-pikes, and such like, and cleared our deck of them twice. However, to cut this melancholy part of our story, our ship being disabled, and three of our men killed, and eight wounded, we were obliged to yield, and were carricd all prisoners into Sallee, a port belonging to the Moors.

The usage I had there was not so dreadful as at first I apprehended, nor was I carried up the country to the Emperor of Morocco's court, as the rest of our men were, but I was kept by the captain of the rover as his own prize, and made his slave, being young and nimble and fit for his business. At this surprising change of my circumstances from a merchant to a miserable slave, I was perfectly overwhelmed; and now I looked back upon my father's prophetic discourse to me, that I should be miserable, and have none to relieve me, which I thought was now so effectually brought to pass that it could not be worse; that now the hand of Heaven had overtaken me, and I was undone without redemption. But alas! This was but a taste of the misery I was to go through, as will appear in the sequel of this story.

I meditated nothing but my escape, and what method I might take to effect it, but found no way that had the least probability in it; so that for two years, though I often pleased myself with the imagination, yet I never had the least encouraging prospect of putting it in practice.

After about two years an odd circumstance presented itself, which put the old thought of making some attempt for my liberty again in my head. My patron still had the longboat of our ship, and he ordered his carpenter to build a little stateroom or cabin in the middle of the longboat, like that of a barge, with a place to stand behind it to steer and haul home the main-sheet, and room before for a hand or two to stand and work the sails; she sailed with that we call a shoulder-of-mutton sail; and the boom gibed over the top of the cabin, which lay very snug and low, and had in it room for him to lie, with a slave or two, and a table to eat on, with some small lockers to put in some bottles of such liquor as he thought fit to drink; and particularly his bread, rice, and coffee.

We went frequently out with this boat fishing, and as I was most dextrous to catch fish for him, he never went without me. It happened that he had arranged to go out in this boat, either for pleasure or for fish, with two or three Moors of some distinction in that place, and for whom he had provided extraordinarily; and had therefore sent on board the boat, overnight, a larger store of provisions than ordinary; and had ordered me to get ready three guns with powder and shot, which were on board his ship; for they designed some sport of fowling as well as fishing.

I got all things ready as he had directed, and waited the next morning with the boat washed clean, and everything to accommodate his guests; when by and by my patron came on board alone, and told me his guests had put off going, upon some business that fell out, and ordered me with a Moor, one of his kinsmen, and a young Maresco slave, to go out with the boat and catch them some fish, for his friends were to sup at his house; and commanded that as soon as I had got some fish I should bring it home to his house; all which I prepared to do.

This moment my former notions of deliverance darted into my thoughts, for now I found I was like to have a little ship at my command; and my master being gone, I prepared to furnish myself, not for a fishing business, but for a voyage; though I knew not, neither did I so much as consider whither I should steer; for anywhere to get out of that place was my way.

My first contrivance was to make a pretence to speak to this Moor, to get something for our subsistence on board; for I told him we must not presume to eat of our patron's bread; he said that was true; so he brought a large basket of rusk or biscuit of their kind, and three jars with fresh water into the boat; I knew where my patron's case of bottles stood, which it was evident by the make were taken out of some English prize; and I conveyed them into the boat while the Moor was on shore, as if they had been there before, for our master: I conveyed also a great lump of beeswax into the boat, which weighed above half a hundredweight, with a parcel of twine or thread, a hatchet, a saw and a hammer, all which were of great use to us afterwards; especially the wax to make candles. Another trick I tried upon him, which he innocently came into also; his name was Ismael, who they call Muly or Moely; so I called to him, 'Moely,' said I, 'our patron's guns are on board the boat, can you not get a little powder and shot? It may be we may kill some fowl for ourselves, for I know he keeps the gunner's stores in the ship.' 'Yes,' says he, 'I'll bring some,' and accordingly he brought a great leather pouch which held about a pound and half of powder, or rather more; and another with shot, that had five or six pound, with some bullets; and put all into the boat. At the same time I had found some powder of my master's in the great cabin, with which I filled one of the large bottles in the case, which was almost empty; pouring what was in it into another: and thus furnished with every thing needful, we sailed out of the port to fish. The castle which is at the entrance of the port knew who we were, and took no notice of us; and we were not above a mile out of the port before we hauled in our sail and set us down to fish. The wind blew from the NNE, which was contrary to my desire; for had it blown southerly I had been sure to have made the coast of Spain, and at least reached the bay of Cadiz; but my resolutions were, blow which way it would, I would be gone from that horrid place where I was, and leave the rest to fate.

After we had fished some time and caught nothing (for when I had fish on my hook, I would not pull them up, that he might not see them), I said to the Moor, 'This will not do, our master will not be thus served, we must stand farther off.' He, thinking no harm, agreed, and being in the head of the boat set the sails; and as I had the helm I run the boat out a league farther, and then brought her too as if I would fish; when giving the boy the helm, I stepped forward to where the Moor was, and making as if I stooped for something behind him, I took him by surprise and tossed him clear overboard into the sea; he rose immediately, for he swam like a cork, and called to me, begged to be taken in, told me he would go all over the world with me; he swam so strong after the boat that he would have reached me very quickly, there being but little wind; upon which I stepped into the cabin, and fetching one of the fowling-pieces, I presented it at him, and told him I had done him no hurt, and if he would be quiet I would do him none; 'but,' said I, 'you swim well enough to reach to the shore, and the sea is calm, make the best of your way to shore and I will do you no harm, but if you come near the boat I'll shoot you through the head; for I am resolved to have my liberty'; so he turned himself about and swam for the shore, and I make no doubt but he reached it with ease, for he was an excellent swimmer.

When he was gone I turned to the boy, who they called Xury, and said to him, 'Xury, if you will be faithful to me I'll make you a great man, but if you will not swear to be true to me, I must throw you into the sea too.' The boy smiled in my face and spoke so innocently that I could not mistrust him; and swore to be faithful to me, and go all over the world with me.

While I was in view of the Moor that was swimming, I stood out directly to sea with the boat, that they might think me gone towards the Straits of Gibraltar (as indeed anyone that had been in their wits must have been supposed to do), for who would have supposed we were sailed on to the southward to the truly Barbarian coast,

where whole nations of negroes were sure to sur-
round us with their canoes, and destroy us; where
we could never once go on shore but we should be
devoured by savage beasts, or merciless savages?

But as soon as it grew dusk in the evening, I
changed my course, and steered directly south
and by east, bending my course a little toward the
east, that I might keep in with the shore; and
having a fair fresh wind, and a smooth quiet sea, I
made such sail that I believe by the next day at
three o'clock in the afternoon, when I first made
the land, I could not be less than 150 miles south
of Sallee; quite beyond the Emperor of Morocco's
dominions, or indeed of any other king thereabouts, for we saw no people.

Yet such was the fright I had taken at the
Moors, and the dreadful apprehensions I had of
falling into their hands, that I would not stop, or
go on shore, or come to anchor (the wind continuing fair), till I had sailed in that manner five days;
then I ventured to make to the coast, and came
to anchor in the mouth of a little river, I knew
not what, or where; neither what latitude, what
country, what nations, or what river: I neither
saw, or desired to see, any people; the principal
thing I wanted was fresh water. We came into this
creek in the evening, resolving to swim on shore
as soon as it was dark, and discover the country;
but as soon as it was quite dark, we heard such
dreadful noises of the barking, roaring, and howl-
ing of wild creatures, of we knew not what kinds,

that the poor boy was ready to die with fear, and begged of me not to go to shore till day. 'Well, Xury,' said I, 'then I won't, but it may be we may see men by day, who will be as bad to us as those lions.' 'Then we give them the shoot gun,' says Xury, laughing, 'make them run wey'; such English Xury spoke by conversing among us slaves. However, I was glad to see the boy so cheerful, and I gave him a dram (out of our patron's case of bottles) to cheer him up. After all, Xury's advice was good, and I took it. We dropped our little anchor and lay still all night; I say still, for we slept none! For in two or three hours we saw vast great creatures (we knew not what to call them) of many sorts, come down to the sea-shore and run into the water, wallowing and washing themselves for the pleasure of cooling themselves; and they made such hideous howlings and yellings, that I never indeed heard the like.

This convinced me that there was no going on shore for us in the night upon that coast, and how to venture on shore in the day was another question too; for to have fallen into the hands of any of the savages had been as bad as to have fallen into the hands of lions and tigers; at least we were equally apprehensive of the danger of it.

Be that as it would, we were obliged to go on shore somewhere or other for water, for we had not a pint left in the boat; when or where to get to it was the point. Xury said, if I would let him go on shore with one of the jars, he would find if there was any water and bring some to me. I asked him why he would go; why I should not go and he stay in the boat; the boy answered with so much affection that made me love him ever after. Says he, 'If wild mans come, they eat me, you go wey.' 'Well, Xury,' said I, 'we will both go, and if the wild mans come we will kill them, they shall eat neither of us.'

We took the boat in as near the shore as we thought was proper, and so waded on shore, carrying nothing but our arms and two jars for water.

I did not care to go out of sight of the boat, fearing the coming of canoes with savages down the river; but the boy seeing a low place about a mile up the country rambled to it; and by and by I saw him come running towards me. I thought he was pursued by some savage, or frightened by some wild beast, and I ran towards him to help him, but when I came nearer to him, I saw something hanging over his shoulders which was a creature that he had shot, like a hare but different in colour, and longer legs; however, we were very glad of it, and it was very good meat; but the great joy that poor Xury came with, was to tell me he had found good water and seen no wild mans.

As I had been one voyage to this coast before, I knew very well that the islands of the Canaries, and the Cape de Verd Islands also, lay not far off from the coast. But as I had no instruments to take an observation to know what latitude we were in, and did not exactly know, or at least remember, what latitude they were in, I knew not where to look for them, or when to stand off to sea towards them; otherwise I might now easily have found some of these islands. But my hope was, that if I stood along this coast till I came to that part where the English traded, I should find some of their vessels upon their usual design of trade, that would relieve and take us in.

By the best of my calculation, that place where I now was, must be that country which, lying between the Emperor of Morocco's dominions and the negro's, lies waste and uninhabited, except by wild beasts; and indeed for near an hundred miles together upon this coast, we saw nothing but a vast uninhabited country by day, and heard nothing but howlings and roaring of wild beasts by night.

Once or twice in the daytime I thought I saw the high top of the mountain Teneriffe in the Canaries, and had a great mind to venture out in hopes of reaching thither; but having tried twice I was forced in again by contrary winds, the sea also going too high for my little vessel, so I resolved to pursue my first design and keep along the shore.

Several times I was obliged to land for fresh water after we had left this place; and once we had to kill a lion. This was game indeed to us, but this was no food, and I was very sorry to lose three charges of powder and shot upon a creature that was good for nothing to us.

I bethought myself, however, that perhaps the skin of him might one way or other be of some value to us, and I resolved to take off his skin if I could. So Xury and I went to work with him; but Xury was much the better workman at it, for I knew very ill how to do it. Indeed, it took us the whole day, but at last we got off the hide of him, and spreading it on the top of our cabin, the sun effectually dried it in two days' time, and it after-wards served me to lie upon.

After this stop we made on to the southward continually for ten or twelve days, living very sparing on our provisions, which began to abate very much, and going no oftener into the shore than we were obliged to for fresh water; my design in this was to reach anywhere about the Cape de Verd, where I was in hopes to meet with some European ship, and if I did not, I knew not what course I had to take, but to seek out for the islands, or perish there among the negroes. I knew that all the ships from Europe, which sailed either to the coast or Guinea, or to Brasil, or to the East Indies, made this cape or those islands; and in a word, I put the whole of my fortune upon this single point, either that I must meet with some ship, or must perish.

So we continued for ten more days. Then on the eleventh day, as I was very pensive, I stepped into the cabin and sat me down, Xury having the helm, when on a sudden the boy cried out, 'Master, master, a ship with a sail,' and the foolish boy was frightened out of his wits, thinking it must needs be some of his master's ships sent to pursue us, when I knew we were far enough out of their reach. I jumped out of the cabin, and immediately saw not only the ship, but that it was a Portuguese ship.

With all the sail I could make, I found I should not be able to come in their way, but that they would be gone by, before I could make any signal to them; but after I had put on as much sail as possible, and began to despair, they it seems saw me by the help of their perspective-glasses, and that it was some European boat, which as they supposed must belong to some ship that was lost, so they shortened sail to let me come up.

They asked me what I was, in Portuguese, and in Spanish, and in French, but I understood none of them; but at last a Scots sailor who was on board called to me, and I answered him, and told him I was an Englishman, that I had made my escape out of slavery from the Moors at Sallee; then they bade me come on board, and very kindly took me in, and all my goods.

3

It was an inexpressible joy to me, as anyone will believe, that I was thus delivered, as I esteemed it, from such a miserable and almost hopeless condition as I was in, and I immediately offered all I had to the captain of the ship, as a return for my deliverance; but he generously told me he would take nothing from me, but that all I had should be delivered safe to me when I came to the Brasils. 'For,' says he, 'I have saved your life on no other terms than I would be glad to be saved myself, and it may one time or other be my lot to be taken up in the same condition; besides,' said he, 'when I carry you to the Brasils, so great a way from your own country, if I should take from you what you have, you will be starved there, and then I only take away what life I have given.'

As to my boat, it was a very good one, and that he saw, and told me he would buy it of me for the ship's use, and asked me what I would have for it. I told him he had been so generous to me in everything, that I could not put any price on the boat, but left it entirely to him, upon which he told me he would give me a note of his hand to pay me 80 pieces of eight for it at Brasil, and when it came there, if anyone offered to give more he would make it up; he offered me also 60 pieces of eight more for my boy Xury, which I was loath to take, not that I was not willing to let the captain have him, but I was very loath to sell the poor boy's liberty, who had assisted me so faithfully in procuring my own. However, when I let him know my reason, he owned it to be just, and offered me this compromise, that he would give the boy an obligation to set him free in ten years, if he turned Christian; upon this, and Xury saying he was willing to go to him, I let the captain have him.

We had a very good voyage to the Brasils, and arrived in All-Saints' Bay in about twenty-two days after. And now I was once more delivered from the most miserable of all conditions of life, and what to do next with myself I was now to consider.

The generous treatment the captain gave me, I can never enough remember; he would take nothing of me for my passage, gave me forty ducats for the lion's skin which I had in my boat, and caused everything I had in the ship to be punctually delivered me, and what I was willing to sell he bought, such as the case of bottles, two of my guns, and a piece of the lump of beeswax, for I had made candles of the rest; in a word, I made about 220 pieces of eight of all my cargo, and with this stock I went on shore in the Brasils.

I had not been long here, but being recommended to the house of a good honest man like himself, who had a plantation, I lived with him some time, and acquainted myself by that means with the manner of their planting and making of sugar; and seeing how well the planters lived, and how they grew rich suddenly, I resolved, if I could get licence to settle there, I would turn planter among them, resolving in the meantime to find out some way to get my money which I had left in London remitted to me. To this purpose getting a kind of letter of naturalization, I purchased as much land that was uncured as my money would reach, and formed a plan for my plantation and settlement.

For two years I could do little more than plant for food, but in the third year my fortunes rose. I was able to plant some tobacco, and my friend, the Portuguese captain, brought for me from England a servant and some cargo, purchased with half of the money I had left in London; which being of good English manufacture, I was able to sell at great profit.

But as abused prosperity is oftentimes made the very means of our greatest adversity, so was it with me. I went on the next year with great success in my plantation; and now increasing in business and in wealth, my head began to be full of projects and undertakings beyond my reach; such as are indeed often the ruin of the best heads in business.

Had I continued in the station I was now in, I had room for all the happy things to have yet befallen me, for which my father so earnestly recommended a quiet retired life, and which he had so sensibly described the middle station of life to be full of; but other things attended me, and I was still to be the wilful agent of all my own miseries.

As I had once done thus in my breaking away from my parents, so I could not be content now, but I must go and leave the happy view I had of being a rich and thriving man in my new plantation, only to pursue a rash and immoderate desire of rising faster than the nature of the thing admitted; and thus I cast myself down again into the deepest gulf of human misery that ever man fell into.

To come then by degrees to the particulars of this part of my story; you may suppose, that having now lived almost four years in the Brasils, and beginning to thrive and prosper very well upon my plantation, I had not only learned the language, but had contracted acquaintance and friendship among my fellow-planters, as well as among the merchants at St Salvadore, which was our port; and that in my discourses among them, I had frequently given them an account of my two voyages to the coast of Guinea, the manner of trading with the negroes there, and how easy it was to purchase upon the coast, for trifles, such as beads, toys, knives, scissors, hatchets, bits of glass, and the like, not only gold dust, elephants' teeth, etc., but negroes, for the service of the Brasils, in great numbers.

They listened always very attentively to my discourses on these heads, but especially to that part which related to buying negroes, which was a trade at that time not only not far entered into, but as far as it was, had been carried on by the permission of the kings of Spain and Portugal, and was subject to monopoly, so that few negroes were brought, and those excessive dear.

It happened, being in company with some merchants and planters of my acquaintance, and talking of those things very earnestly, three of them came to me the next morning, and told me they had been musing very much upon what I had discoursed with them of, the last night, and they came to make a secret proposal to me; and after enjoining me secrecy, they told me that they had a mind to fit out a ship to go to Guinea, that they had all plantations as well as I, and were straitened for nothing so much as servants; that as it was a trade that could not be carried on, because they could not publicly sell the negroes when they came home, so they desired to make but one voyage, to bring the negroes on shore privately, and divide them among their own plantations; and in a word, the question was, whether I would go to manage the trading part upon the coast of Guinea. And they offered me that I should have my equal share of the negroes without providing any part of the stock.

This was a fair proposal, it must be confessed, had it been made to anyone that had not had a settlement and plantation of his own to look after, which was in a fair way of coming to be very considerable, and with a good stock upon it. But for me that was thus entered and established, and had nothing to do but go on as I had begun for three or four years more, and to have sent for the other hundred pound from England, and who in that time, and with that little addition, could scarce have failed of being worth three or four thousand pounds sterling, and that increasing too; for me to think of such a voyage, was the most preposterous thing that ever man in such circumstances could be guilty of.

But I that was born to be my own destroyer, could no more resist the offer than I could restrain my first rambling designs, when my father's good counsel was lost upon me. In a word, I told them I would go with all my heart, if they would undertake to look after my plantation in my absence, and would dispose of it to such as I should direct if I miscarried. I also made the owner of the neighbouring plantation the partner of my plantation. Accordingly the ship being fitted out, and the cargo furnished, and all things done as by agreement, by my partners in the voyage, I went on board in an evil hour, the first of September, 1659, being eight years to the day from when I left my father and mother at Hull, in order to act the rebel to their authority, and the fool to my own interest.

The same day I went on board we set sail, standing away to the northward upon our own coast, with design later to stretch over for the African coast. We had very good weather, only excessive hot, all the way upon our own coast. In this course we passed the equator in about twelve days' time, when a violent hurricane took us quite out of our knowledge; it blew in such a terrible manner, that for twelve days together we could do nothing but drive, and scudding away before it, let it carry us whither fate and the fury of the winds directed; and during these twelve days, I need not say that I expected every day to be swallowed up, nor indeed did any in the ship expect to save their lives.

In this distress, we had, besides the terror of the storm, one of our men died of the fever, and one man and the boy washed over board; about the twelfth day the weather abating a little, the master made an observation as well as he could, and found that he was in the north part of Brasil, beyond the river Amozones, toward the river Oronoque, commonly called the Great River, and began to consult with me what course he should take, for the ship was leaky and very much disabled, and he was for going directly back to the coast of Brasil.

I was positively against that, and looking over the charts of the sea-coast of America with him, we concluded there was no inhabited country for us to have recourse to till we came within the circle of the Carribee-Islands, and therefore resolved to stand away for Barbadoes, which we might easily perform, as we hoped, in about fifteen days' sail; whereas we could not possibly make our voyage to the coast of Africa without some assistance, both to our ship and to ourselves.

With this design we changed our course and steered away in order to reach some of our English islands, where I hoped for relief; but our voyage was otherwise determined, for a second storm came upon us, which carried us away with the same impetuosity westward, and drove us so out of the very way of all human commerce, that had all our lives been saved, as to the sea, we were rather in danger of being devoured by savages than ever returning to our own country.

In this distress, the wind still blowing very hard, one of our men early in the morning cried out, 'Land!' and we had no sooner run out of the cabin to look out in hopes of seeing whereabouts in the world we were, but the ship struck upon a sand, and in a moment, her motion being so stopped, the sea broke over her in such a manner that we expected we should all have perished immediately.

It is not easy for anyone, who has not been in the like condition, to describe or conceive the consternation of men in such circumstances; we knew not where we were, or upon what land it was we were driven, whether an island or the main, whether inhabited or not inhabited; and as the rage of the wind was still great, though rather less than at first, we could not so much as hope to have the ship hold many minutes without breaking in pieces, unless the winds by a kind of miracle should turn immediately about. In a word, we sat looking upon one another, and expecting death every moment, and every man acting accordingly, as preparing for another world, for there was little or nothing more for us to do in this; that which was our present comfort, and all the comfort we had was, that contrary to our expectation the ship did not break yet, and that the master said the wind began to abate.

In this distress the mate of our vessel lays hold of the boat, and with the help of the rest of the men, they got her slung over the ship's side, and getting all into her, let go, and committed ourselves, being eleven in number, to God's mercy and the wild sea; for though the storm was abated considerably, yet the sea went dreadful high upon the shore.

And now our case was very dismal indeed; for we all saw plainly, that the sea went so high that the boat could not live, and that we should be inevitably drowned. As to making sail, we had none, nor, if we had, could we have done anything with it: so we worked at the oar towards the land, though with heavy hearts, like men going to execution; for we all knew that when the boat came nearer the shore, she would be dashed in a thousand pieces by the breakers.

After we had rowed, or rather driven, about a league and a half, as we reckoned it, a raging wave, mountain-like, came rolling astern of us; it took us with such a fury, that it overset the boat at once; and separating us as well from the boat as from one another, gave us not time hardly to say, O God! For we were all swallowed up in a moment.

Nothing can describe the confusion of thought which I felt when I sunk into the water; for though I swam very well, yet I could not deliver myself from the waves so as to draw breath, till that wave having driven me, or rather carried me a vast way on towards the shore, and having spent itself, went back, and left me upon the land almost dry, but half-dead with the water I took in. I had so much presence of mind as well as breath left, that seeing myself nearer land than I expected, I got upon my feet, and endeavoured to make on towards the land as fast as I could, before another wave should return, and take me up again. But I soon found it was impossible to avoid it; for I saw the sea come after me as high as a great hill, and as furious as an enemy which I had no means or strength to contend with; my business was to hold my breath, and raise myself upon the water, if I could; and so by swimming to preserve my breathing, and pilot myself towards the shore, if possible; my greatest concern now being, that the sea, as it would carry me a great way towards the shore when it came on, might not carry me back again with it when it gave back towards the sea.

The wave that came upon me again, buried me at once twenty or thirty foot deep in its own body; and I could feel myself carried with a mighty force and swiftness towards the shore a very great way; but I held my breath, and assisted myself to swim still forward with all my might. I was ready to burst with holding my breath, when, as I felt myself rising up, so to my immediate relief, I found my head and hands shoot out above the surface of the water; and though it was not two seconds of time that I could keep myself so, yet it relieved me greatly, gave me breath and new courage. I was covered again with water a good while, but not so long but I held it out; and finding the water had spent itself, and began to return, I struck forward against the return of the waves, and felt ground again with my feet. I stood still a few moments to recover breath, and till the water went from me, and then took to my heels, and ran with what strength I had farther towards the shore. But neither would this deliver me from the fury of the sea, which came pouring in after me again, and twice more I was lifted up by the waves and carried forwards as before, the shore being very flat.

The last time of these two had well near been fatal to me; for the sea having hurried me along as before, landed me, or rather dashed me, against a piece of a rock, and that with such force as it left me senseless, and indeed helpless as to my own deliverance; for the blow taking my side and breast, beat the breath as it were quite out of my body; and had it returned again immediately, I must have been strangled in the water; but I recovered a little before the return of the waves, and seeing I should be covered again with the water, I resolved to hold fast by a piece of the rock, and so to hold my breath, if possible, till the wave went back; now as the waves were not so high as at first, being nearer land, I held my hold till the wave abated, and then fetched another run, which brought me so near the shore, that the next wave, though it went over me, yet did not so swallow me up as to carry me away, and the next run I took, I got to land, where, to my great comfort, I clambered up the shore and sat me down upon the grass, free from danger, and quite out of the reach of the water.

## 4

I was now landed and safe on shore, and began to look up and thank God that my life was saved in a case wherein there was some minutes before scarce any room to hope. I walked about on the shore, wrapped up in the contemplation of my deliverance, making a thousand gestures and motions which I cannot describe, reflecting upon all my comrades that were drowned, and that there should not be one soul saved but myself, for, as for them, I never saw them afterwards, or any sign of them, except three of their hats, one cap, and two shoes that were not fellows.

I cast my eyes to the stranded vessel, when the breaking and froth of the sea being so big, I could hardly see it, it lay so far off, and considered, Lord! How was it possible I could get on shore?

After I had solaced my mind with the comfortable part of my condition, I began to look round me to see what kind of place I was in, and what was next to be done, and I soon found my comforts abate, and that in a word I had a dreadful deliverance: for I was wet, had no clothes to change into, nor anything either to eat or drink to comfort me, neither did I see any prospect before me, but that of perishing with hunger, or being devoured by wild beasts; and that which was particularly afflicting to me was that I had no weapon either to hunt and kill any creature for my sustenance, or to defend myself against any other creature that might desire to kill me for theirs. In a word, I had nothing about me but a knife, a tobacco-pipe, and a little tobacco in a box; this was all my provision, and this threw me into such terrible agonies of mind, that for a while I ran about like a madman. Night coming upon me, I began with a heavy heart to consider what would be my lot if there were any ravenous beasts in that country, seeing at night they always come abroad for their prey.

All the remedy that offered to my thoughts at that time was to get up into a thick bushy tree like a fir, but thorny, which grew near me, and where I resolved to sit all night, and consider the next day what death I should die, for as yet I saw no prospect of life; I walked about a furlong from the shore, to see if I could find any fresh water to drink, which I did, to my great joy; and having drank and put a little tobacco in my mouth to prevent hunger, I went to the tree, and getting up into it, endeavoured to place myself so that if I should sleep I might not fall; and having cut me a short stick, like a truncheon, for my defence, I took up my lodging, and having been excessively fatigued, I fell fast asleep.

When I waked it was broad day, the weather clear, and the storm abated, so that the sea did not rage and swell as before: but that which surprised me most was that the ship was lifted off in the night from the sand where she lay, by the swelling of the tide, and was driven up almost as far as the rock which I first mentioned, where I had been so bruised by being dashed against it; this being within about a mile from the shore where I was, and the ship seeming to stand upright still, I wished myself on board, that, at least, I might save some necessary things for my use.

When I came down from my apartment in the tree, I looked about me again, and the first thing I found was the boat, which lay as the wind and the sea had tossed her up upon the land, about two miles on my right hand. I walked as far as I could upon the shore to have got to her, but found a neck or inlet of water between me and the boat, which was about half a mile broad, so I came back for the present, being more intent upon getting at the ship, where I hoped to find something for my present subsistence.

A little after noon I found the sea very calm, and the tide ebbed so far out that I could come within a quarter of a mile of the ship; and here I found a fresh renewing of my grief, for I saw evidently, that if we had kept on board, we had been all safe, that is to say, we had all got safe on shore, and I had not been so miserable as to be left entirely destitute of all comfort and company, as I now was; this forced tears from my eyes again, but as there was little relief in that, I resolved, if possible, to get to the ship, so I pulled off my clothes, for the weather was hot to extremity, and took to the water.

I was able to make eleven trips to the boat, and built rafts to bring the goods I wanted back to the shore. In short, I took from the boat everything that could be useful to me in my present condition – wood, cable, string, the few tools I could find, a grindstone, nails, guns and powder and shot, swords, food and drink, clothes, a hammock, some bedding, and some canvas, with which I made myself a tent. Apart from these I got several things of less value, but not less useful to me, in particular pens, ink and paper, compasses, and three Bibles. But preparing the twelfth time to go on board, I found the wind begin to rise; however, at low water I went on board, and though I thought I had rummaged the cabin so effectually, that nothing more could be found, yet I discovered a locker with drawers in it, in one of which I found two or three razors, and one pair of large scissors, with some ten or a dozen of good knives and forks; in another I found about thirty-six pounds value in money, some European coin, some Brasil, some pieces of eight, some gold, some silver.

I smiled to myself at the sight of this money. 'What art thou good for?' said I aloud. 'Thou are not worth to me, no, not the taking off of the ground; one of those knives is worth all this heap; I have no manner of use for thee; remain where thou art, and go to the bottom as a creature whose life is not worth saving.' However, upon second thoughts, I took it away, and wrapping all this in a piece of canvas, I began to think of making another raft, but while I was preparing this, I found the sky overcast, and the wind began to rise, and in a quarter of an hour it blew a fresh gale from the shore; it presently occurred to me that it was in vain to pretend to make a raft with the wind off shore, and that it was my business to be gone before the tide of flood began, otherwise I might not be able to reach the shore at all. Accordingly I let myself down into the water, and swam across the channel which lay between the ship and the sands, and even that with difficulty enough, partly with the weight of the things I had about me, and partly the roughness of the water, for the wind rose very hastily, and before it was quite high water it blew a storm.

But I got home to my little tent, where I lay with all my wealth about me very secure. It blew very hard all that night, and in the morning when I looked out, behold, no more ship was to be seen; I was a little surprised, but recovered myself with this satisfactory reflection, that I had lost no time, nor abated no diligence to get everything out of her that could be useful to me, and that indeed there was little left in her that I was able to bring away if I had more time.

I now gave over any more thoughts of the ship, or of anything out of her, except what might drive on shore from her wreck, as indeed divers pieces of her afterwards did; but those things were of small use to me.

My thoughts were now wholly employed about securing myself against either savages, if any should appear, or wild beasts, if any were in the island; and I had many thoughts of the method how to do this, and what kind of dwelling to make, whether I should make me a cave in the earth, or a tent upon the earth: and, in short, I resolved upon both, the manner and description of which it may not be improper to give an account of.

I soon found the place I was in was not for my settlement, particularly because it was upon a low marshy ground near the sea, and I believed would not be wholesome, and more particularly because there was no fresh water near it, so I resolved to find a more healthy and more convenient spot of ground.

I consulted several things in my situation which I found would be proper for me: first, health and fresh water I just now mentioned; secondly, shelter from the heat of the sun; thirdly, security from ravenous creatures, whether men or beasts; fourthly, a view to the sea, that if God sent any ship in sight, I might not lose any advantage for my deliverance, of which I was not willing to banish all my expectation yet.

In search of a place proper for this, I found a little plain on the side of a rising hill, whose front towards this little plain was steep as a house-side, so that nothing could come down upon me from the top; on the side of this rock there was a hollow place worn a little way in like the entrance or door of a cave, but there was not really any cave or way into the rock at all.

On the flat of the green, just before this hollow place, I resolved to pitch my tent. This plain was not above a hundred yards broad, and about twice as long, and lay like a green before my door, and at the end of it descended irregularly every way down into the low grounds by the sea-side. It was on the NNW side of the hill, so that I was sheltered from the heat every day, till it came to a west and by south sun, or thereabouts, which in those countries is near the setting.

Before I set up my tent, I drew a half circle before the hollow place which took in about ten yards in its semi-diameter from the rock, and twenty yards in its diameter, from its beginning and ending.

In this half circle I pitched two rows of strong stakes, driving them into the ground till they stood very firm, the biggest end being out of the ground about five foot and a half, and sharpened on the top. The two rows did not stand above six inches from one another.

Then I took the pieces of cable which I had cut in the ship, and I laid them in rows one upon another, within the circle, between these two rows of stakes, up to the top, placing other stakes in the inside, leaning against them, about two foot and a half high, like a spur to a post, and this fence was so strong that neither man or beast could get into it or over it. This cost me a great deal of time and labour, especially to cut the stakes in the woods, bring them to the place, and drive them into the earth.

The entrance into this place I made to be not by a door, but by a short ladder to go over the top, which ladder, when I was in, I lifted over after me, and so I was completely fenced in, and fortified, as I thought, from all the world and consequently slept secure in the night, which otherwise I could not have done, though, as it appeared afterward, there was no need of all this caution from the enemies that I apprehended danger from.

Into this fence or fortress, with infinite labour, I carried all my riches, all my provisions, ammunition, and stores, of which you have the account above; and I made me a large tent, which, to preserve me from the rains that in one part of the year are very violent there, I made double – one smaller tent within, and one larger tent above it – and covered the uppermost with a large tarpaulin which I had saved among the sails.

And now I lay no more for a while in the bed which I had brought on shore, but in a hammock, which was indeed a very good one, and belonged to the mate of the ship.

Into this tent I brought all my provisions, and everything that would spoil by the wet, and having thus enclosed all my goods, I made up the entrance, which till now I had left open, and so passed and re-passed, as I said, by a short ladder.

When I had done this, I began to work my way into the rock, and bringing all the earth and stones that I dug down out through my tent, I laid them up within my fence in the nature of a terrace, so that it raised the ground within about a foot and a half; and thus I made me a cave just behind my tent, which served me like a cellar to my house.

It cost me much labour and many days before all these things were brought to perfection. I went out at least once every day with my gun, as well to divert myself as to see if I could kill anything fit for food, and as near as I could to acquaint myself with what the island produced. The first time I went out I presently discovered that there were goats in the islands, which was a great satisfaction to me; I soon found that if they saw me in the valleys, though they were upon the rocks, they would run away as in a terrible fright; but if they were feeding in the valleys, and I was upon the rocks, they took no notice of me; their sight was so directed downward, that they did not readily see objects that were above them; so afterward I took this method, I always climbed the rocks first to get above them, and then had frequently a fair mark.

I had a dismal prospect of my condition, for as I was not cast away upon that island without being driven by a violent storm quite out of the course of our intended voyage, and some hundreds of leagues out of the ordinary course of the trade of mankind, I had great reason to consider it as a determination of Heaven, that in this desolate place and in this desolate manner I should end my life.

It was, by my account, the 30th of Sept. when, in the manner as above said, I first set foot upon this horrid island. After I had been there about ten or twelve days, it came into my thoughts that I should lose my reckoning of time and should even forget the Sabbath days from the working days; but to prevent this I cut with my knife upon a large post, in capital letters, and making it into a great cross I set it up on the shore where I first landed, 'I came on shore here on the 30th of Sept. 1659.' Upon the sides of this square post I cut every day a notch with my knife, and every seventh notch was as long again as the rest, and every first day of the month as long again as that long one, and thus I kept my calendar.

Notwithstanding all that I had amassed together, I lacked many tools for life on land. This want of tools made every work I did go on heavily, and it was near a whole year before I had entirely finished my little pale or surrounded habitation.

The stakes, which were as heavy as I could well lift, were a long time in cutting and preparing in the woods, and more by far in bringing home, so that I spent sometimes two days in cutting and bringing home one of those posts, and a third day in driving it into the ground; for which purpose I got a heavy piece of wood at first, but at last bethought myself of an iron crow-bar I had salvaged from the boat, which however, though I found it, yet it made driving those posts very laborious and tedious work.

But what need had I to be concerned at the tediousness of anything I had to do, seeing I had time enough to do it in? Nor had I any other employment if that had been over, at least that I could foresee, except ranging the island to seek for food, which I did more or less every day.

I now began to consider seriously my condition, and the circumstance I was reduced to, and I drew up the state of my affairs in writing, not so much to leave them to any that were to come after me, for I was like to have but few heirs, as to deliver my thoughts from daily poring upon them, and afflicting my mind; and as my reason began now to master my despondency, I began to comfort myself as well as I could, and to set the good against the evil, that I might have something to distinguish my case from worse, and I stated it very impartially, like debtor and creditor, the comforts I enjoyed against the miseries I suffered, thus:

| Evil | Good |
|------|------|
| *I am cast upon a horrible desolate island, void of all hope of recovery.* | *But I am alive, and not drowned as all my ship's company was.* |
| *I am singled out and separated, as it were, from all the world to be miserable.* | *But I am singled out too from all the ship's crew to be spared from death; and He that miraculously saved me from death, can deliver me from this condition.* |
| *I am divided from mankind, a solitaire, one banished from human society.* | *But I am not starved and perishing on a barren place, affording no sustenance.* |
| *I have not clothes to cover me.* | *But I am in a hot climate, where if I had no clothes I could hardly wear them.* |
| *I am without any defence or means to resist any violence of man or beast.* | *But I am cast on an island, where I see no wild beasts to hurt me, as I saw on the coast of Africa; and what if I had been shipwrecked there?* |

*I have no soul to speak to, or relieve me.*

*But God wonderfully sent the ship in near enough to the shore, that I have got out so many necessary things as will either supply my wants, or enable me to supply myself even as long as I live.*

Having now brought my mind a little to relish my condition, and given over looking out to sea to see if I could spy a ship; I say, giving over these things, I began to apply myself to accommodate my way of living, and to make things as easy to me as I could.

I have already described my habitation, which was a tent under the side of a rock, surrounded with a strong pale of posts and cables, but I might now rather call it a wall, for I raised a kind of wall up against it of turfs, about two foot thick on the outside, and after some time, I think it was a year and a half, I raised rafters from it leaning to the rock, and thatched or covered it with branches and such things as I could get to keep out the rain, which I found at some times of the year very violent.

I have already observed how I brought all my goods into this pale, and into the cave which I had made behind me. But I must observe too, that at first this was a confused heap of goods, which as they lay in no order, so they took up all my place, and I had no room to turn myself; so I set myself to enlarge my cave and works farther into the earth, for it was a loose sandy rock, which yielded easily to the labour I bestowed on it, and so when I found I was pretty safe as to beasts of prey, I worked sideways to the right hand into the rock, and then turning to the right again, worked quite out and made me a door to come out, on the outside of my fortification.

This gave me not only egress and regress, as it were a back way to my tent and to my storehouse, but gave me room to stow my goods.

And now I began to apply myself to make such necessary things as I found I most wanted, as particularly a chair and a table for without these I was not able to enjoy the few comforts I had in the world; I could not write, or eat, or do several things with so much pleasure without a table.

So I went to work; I had never handled a tool in my life, and yet in time, by labour, application, and contrivance, I found at last that I wanted nothing but I could have made it, especially if I had had tools; however, I made abundance of things, even without tools, and some with no more tools than an adze and a hatchet, which perhaps were never made that way before, and that with infinite labour. For example, if I wanted a board, I had no other way but to cut down a tree, set it on an edge before me, and hew it flat on either side with my axe, till I had brought it to be thin as a plank, and then dub it smooth with my adze. It is true, by this method I could make but one board out of a whole tree, but this I had no remedy for but patience, any more than I had for the prodigious deal of time and labour which it took me up to make a plank or board. But my time or labour was little worth, and so it was as well employed one way as another.

However, I made me a table and a chair, as I observed above, in the first place, and this I did out of short pieces of boards that I brought on my raft from the ship. But when I had wrought out some boards, as above, I made large shelves of the breadth of a foot and a half one over another, all along one side of my cave, to lay all my tools, nails, and iron-work, and in a word, to separate everything at large in their places, so that I could come easily at them; I knocked pieces into the wall of the rock to hang my guns and all things that would hang up.

And now it was when I began to keep a journal of every day's employment, for indeed at first I was in too much hurry, and not only hurry as to labour, but in too much discomposure of mind, and my journal would have been full of many dull things. For example, I might have said thus: 'Sept. the 30th. After I got to shore and had escaped drowning, instead of being thankful to God for my deliverance, having first vomited with the great quantity of salt water which had got into my stomach, and recovering myself a little, I ran about the shore, wringing my hands and beating my head and face, exclaiming at my misery, and crying out, I was undone, undone, till tired and faint I was forced to lie down on the ground to repose, but dared not sleep for fear of being devoured.'

Some days after this, and after I had been on board the ship, and got all that I could out of her, yet I could not forbear getting up to the top of a little mountain and looking out to sea in hopes of seeing a ship, then fancy at a vast distance I spied a sail, please myself with the hopes of it, and then after looking steadily till I was almost blind, lose it quite, and sit down and weep like a child, and thus increase my misery by my folly.

But having got over these things in some measure, and having settled my household stuff and habitation, made me a table and a chair, and all as handsome about me as I could, I began to keep my journal, of which I shall here give you a copy (though in it will be told all these particulars over again) as long as it lasted, for having no more ink I was forced to leave it off.

## 5

September 30, 1659. I, poor miserable Robinson Crusoe, being shipwrecked during a dreadful storm, came on shore on this dismal, unfortunate island, which I called the Island of Despair, all the rest of the ship's company being drowned, and myself almost dead.

All the rest of that day I spent in afflicting myself at the dismal circumstances I was brought to; I had neither food, house, clothes, weapon, or place to fly to, and in despair of any relief, saw nothing but death before me, either that I should be devoured by wild beasts, murdered by savages, or starved to death for want of food. At the approach of night, I slept in a tree for fear of wild creatures, but slept soundly though it rained all night.

October 1. In the morning I saw to my great surprise the ship had floated with the high tide, and was driven on shore again much nearer the island, which as it was some comfort on the one hand, for seeing her sit upright, and not broken to pieces, I hoped, if the wind abated, I might get on board, and get some food and necessaries out of her for my relief; so on the other hand, it renewed my grief at the loss of my comrades, who I imagined if we had all stayed on board might have saved the ship, or at least that they would not have been all drowned as they were; and that had the men been saved, we might perhaps have built us a boat out of the ruins of the ship, to have carried us to some other part of the world. I spent a great part of this day in perplexing myself on these things; but at length seeing the ship almost dry, I went upon the sand as near as I could, and then swam on board; this day also it continued raining, though with no wind at all.

From the 1st of October to the 24th. All these days entirely spent in many several voyages to get all I could out of the ship, which I brought on shore, every tide of flood, upon rafts. Much rain also in these days, though with some intervals of fair weather: but, it seems, this is the rainy season.

Oct. 25. It rained all night and all day, with some gusts of wind, during which time the ship broke in pieces, the wind blowing a little harder than before, and was no more to be seen, except the wreck of her, and that only at low water. I spent this day in covering and securing the goods which I had saved, that the rain might not spoil them.

Oct. 26. I walked about the shore almost all day to find out a place to fix my habitation, greatly concerned to secure myself from an attack in the night, either from wild beasts or men. Towards night I fixed upon a proper place under a rock, and marked out a semicircle for my encampment, which I resolved to strengthen with a work, wall, or fortification made of double stakes, lined within with cables, and without with turf.

From the 26th to the 30th I worked very hard in carrying all my goods to my new habitation, though some part of the time it rained exceeding hard.

The 31st in the morning I went out into the island with my gun to look for some food, and discover the country, when I killed a she-goat, and her kid followed me home, which I afterwards killed also because it would not feed.

November 1. I set up my tent under a rock, and lay there for the first night, making it as large as I could with stakes driven in to swing my hammock upon.

Nov. 2. I set up all my chests and boards, and the pieces of timber which made my rafts, and with them formed a fence round me, a little within the place I had marked out for my fortification.

Nov. 3. I went out with my gun and killed two fowls like ducks, which were very good food. In the afternoon went to work to make me a table.

Nov. 4. This morning I began to order my times of work, of going out with my gun, time of sleep, and time of diversion; every morning I walked out with my gun for two or three hours if it did not rain, then employed myself to work till about eleven o'clock, then eat what I had to live on, and from twelve to two I lay down to sleep, the weather being excessive hot, and then in the evening to work again. The working part of this day and of the next were wholly employed in making my table, for I was yet but a very sorry workman, though time and necessity made me a complete natural mechanic soon after, as I believe it would do anyone else.

Nov. 6. After my morning walk I went to work with my table again, and finished it, though not to my liking; nor was it long before I learned to mend it.

Nov. 7. Now it began to be settled fair weather. The 7th, 8th, 9th, 10th, and part of the 12th (for the 11th was Sunday) I took wholly up to make me a chair, and with much ado brought it to a tolerable shape, but never to please me, and even in the making I pulled it in pieces several times. *Note*, I soon neglected my keeping Sundays, for omitting my mark for them on my post, I forgot which was which.

Nov. 13. This day it rained, which refreshed me exceedingly, and cooled the earth, but it was accompanied with terrible thunder and lightning, which frightened me dreadfully for fear of my powder; as soon as it was over, I resolved to separate my stock of powder into as many little parcels as possible, that it might not be in danger.

Nov. 14, 15, 16. These three days I spent in making little square chests or boxes, which might hold a pound or two pound, at most, of powder, and so putting the powder in, I stowed it in places as secure and remote from one another as possible. On one of these three days I killed a large bird that was good to eat, but I know not what to call it.

Nov. 17. This day I began to dig behind my tent into the rock to make room for my farther conveniency. *Note*, Three things I wanted exceedingly for this work, a pick-axe, a shovel, and a wheelbarrow or basket; so I desisted from my work, and began to consider how to supply that want and make me some tools; as for a pick-axe, I made use of the iron crows, which were proper enough, though heavy; but the next thing was a shovel or spade; this was so absolutely necessary, that indeed I could do nothing effectually without it, but what kind of one to make I knew not.

Nov. 18. The next day in searching the woods I found a tree of that wood, or like it, which in the Brasils they call the iron tree, for its exceeding hardness; of this, with great labour and almost spoiling my axe, I cut a piece, and brought it home too with difficulty enough, for it was exceeding heavy.

The excessive hardness of the wood, and having no other way, made me a long while upon this machine, for I worked it effectually by little and little into the form of a shovel or spade, the handle exactly shaped like ours in England, only that the broad part having no iron shod upon it at bottom, it would not last me so long; however, it served well enough for the uses which I had occasion to put it to; but never was a shovel, I believe, made after that fashion, or so long in the making.

I was still deficient, for I wanted a basket or a wheelbarrow; a basket I could not make by any means, having no such things as twigs that would bend to make wicker ware, at least none yet found out; and as to a wheelbarrow, I fancied I could make all but the wheel, but that I had no notion of, neither did I know how to go about it; so I gave it over, and so for carrying away the earth which I dug out of the cave, I made me a thing like a hod, which the labourers carry mortar in when they serve the bricklayers.

This was not so difficult to me as the making the shovel; and yet this, and the shovel, and the attempt which I made in vain to make a wheelbarrow, took me up no less than four days; I mean, always excepting my morning walk with my gun, which I seldom failed, and very seldom failed also bringing home something fit to eat.

Nov. 23. My other work having now stood still, because of my making these tools, when they were finished I went on, and working every day, as my strength and time allowed, I spent eighteen days entirely in widening and deepening my cave, that it might hold my goods commodiously.

*Note*, During all this time, I worked to make this room or cave spacious enough to accommodate me as a warehouse, a kitchen, a dining-room, and a cellar; as for my lodging, I kept to the tent, except that sometimes in the wet season of the year, it rained so hard that I could not keep myself dry, which caused me afterwards to cover all my place within my pale with long poles in the form of rafters leaning against the rock, and load them with grass and large leaves of trees like a thatch.

December 10th. I began now to think my cave or vault finished, when on a sudden (it seems I had made it too large) a great quantity of earth fell down from the top and one side, so much, that in short it frightened me, and not without reason too; for if I had been under it I had never wanted a grave-digger. Upon this disaster I had a great deal of work to do over again; for I had the loose earth to carry out, and, which was of more importance, I had the ceiling to prop up, so that I might be sure no more would come down.

Dec. 11. This day I went to work with it accordingly, and got two shores or posts pitched upright to the top, with two pieces of boards across over each post; this I finished the next day; and setting more posts up with boards, in about a week more I had the roof secured, and the posts, standing in rows, served me for partitions to part of my house.

Dec. 17. From this day to the twentieth I placed shelves, and knocked up nails on the posts to hang everything up that could be hung up, and now I began to be in some order within doors.

Dec. 20. Now I carried everything into the cave, and began to furnish my house, and set up some pieces of boards, like a dresser, to order my victuals upon, but boards began to be very scarce with me; also I made me another table.

Dec. 27. Killed a young goat, and lamed another so that I caught it, and led it home on a string; when I had it home, I bound and splintered up its leg, which was broke. *N.B.* I took such care of it that it lived, and the leg grew well, and as strong as ever; but by my nursing it so long it grew tame, and fed upon the little green at my door, and would not go away. This was the first time that I entertained a thought of breeding up some tame creatures, that I might have food when my powder and shot was all spent.

Dec. 28, 29, 30. Great heats and no breeze; so that there was no stirring abroad, except in the evening for food; this time I spent in putting all my things in order within doors.

Jan. 3. I began my fence or wall; which, being still jealous of my being attacked by somebody, I resolved to make very thick and strong.

*NB. This wall being described before, I purposely omit what was said in the Journal; it is sufficient to observe that I was no less time than from the 3rd of January to the 14th of April, working, finishing, and perfecting this wall, though it was no more than about 24 yards in length, being a half circle from one place in the rock to another place about eight yards from it, the door of the cave being in the centre behind it.*

When this wall was finished, and the outside double fenced with a turf-wall raised up close to it, I persuaded myself that if any people were to come on shore there, they would not perceive anything like a habitation; and it was very well I did so, as may be observed hereafter upon a very remarkable occasion.

And now, in the managing my household affairs, I found myself wanting in many things, which I thought at first it was impossible for me to make, as indeed as to some of them it was; for instance, I could never make a cask to be hooped.

In the next place, I was at a great loss for candle; so that as soon as ever it was dark, which was generally by seven o'clock, I was obliged to go to bed. I remembered the lump of beeswax with which I made candles in my African adventure, but I had none of that now; the only remedy I had was, that when I had killed a goat, I saved the tallow, and with a little dish made of clay, which I baked in the sun, to which I added a wick of some oakum, I made me a lamp; and this gave me light, though not a clear, steady light like a candle. In the middle of all my labours it happened, that rummaging my things, I found a little bag, which had been filled with corn for the feeding of poultry, not for this voyage, but before, as I suppose, when the ship came from Lisbon. What little remainder of corn had been in the bag was all devoured by rats, and I saw nothing in the bag but husks and dust; and being willing to have the bag for some other use, I think it was to put powder in, when I divided it for fear of the lightning, or some such use, I shook the husks of corn out of it on one side of my fortification under the rock.

It was a little before the great rains, just now mentioned, that I threw this stuff away, taking no notice of anything, and not so much as remembering that I had thrown anything there; when about a month after, or thereabout, I saw some few stalks of something green shooting out of the ground, which I fancied might be some plant I had not seen; but I was surprised and perfectly astonished, when, after a little longer time, I saw about ten or twelve ears come out, which were perfect green barley.

It is impossible to express the astonishment and confusion of my thoughts on this occasion. When I saw barley grow there, in a climate which I know was not proper for corn, and especially that I knew not how it came there, it startled me strangely, and I began to suggest that God had miraculously caused this grain to grow without any help of seed sown, and that it was so directed purely for my sustenance on that wild, miserable place.

This touched my heart a little, and brought tears out of my eyes, and I began to bless myself that such a prodigy of nature should happen upon my account; and this was the more strange to me, because I saw near it, by the side of the rock, some other straggling stalks, which proved to be stalks of rice, and which I knew, because I had seen it grow in Africa when I was ashore there.

I not only thought these the pure productions of Providence for my support, but not doubting but that there was more in the place, I went all over that part of the island where I had been before, peering in every corner, and under every rock, to look for more of it, but I could not find any; at last it occurred to my thoughts, that I had shook a bag of chickens' food out in that place, and then the wonder began to cease; and I must confess, my religious thankfulness to God's providence began to abate too, upon the discovering that all this was nothing but what was common; though I ought to have been as thankful for such a strange and unforeseen providence, as if it had been miraculous; for it was really the work of Providence that ten or twelve grains of corn should remain unspoiled (when the rats destroyed all the rest) as if it had been dropped from heaven; and that I should throw it out in that particular place, where, it being in the shade of a high rock, it sprang up immediately; whereas, if I had thrown it anywhere else at that time, it had been burnt up and destroyed.

I carefully saved the ears of this corn, you may be sure, in their season, which was about the end of June; and laying up every corn, I resolved to sow them all again, hoping in time to have some quantity sufficient to supply me with bread. But it was not till the fourth year that I could allow myself the least grain of this corn to eat, and even then but sparingly; for I lost all that I sowed the first season by not observing the proper time; for I sowed it just before the dry season, so that it never came up at all, at least not as it would have done.

Besides this barley, there were twenty or thirty stalks of rice, which I preserved with the same care, and whose use was of the same kind or to the same purpose, to make me bread, or rather food; for I found ways to cook it up without baking, though I did that also after some time. But to return to my journal.

I worked excessive hard these three or four months to get my wall done; and the 14th of April I closed it up, contriving to go into it, not by a door, but over the wall by a ladder, that there might be no sign on the outside of my habitation.

April 16. I finished the ladder, so I went up with the ladder to the top, and then pulled it up after me, and let it down in the inside. This was a complete enclosure to me; for within I had room enough, and nothing could come at me from without, unless it could first mount my wall.

May 1. In the morning, looking towards the

sea-side, the tide being low, I saw something on the shore bigger than ordinary, and it looked like a cask; when I came to it, I found a small barrel, and two or three pieces of the wreck of the ship. I examined the barrel and soon found it was a barrel of gunpowder, but it had taken water, and the powder was caked as hard as a stone; however, I rolled it farther on shore for the present.

June 16. Going down to the sea-side, I found a large tortoise or turtle; this was the first I had seen, which it seems was only my misfortune, not any defect of the place, or scarcity; for had I happened to be on the other side of the island, I might have had hundreds of them every day, as I found afterwards; but perhaps had paid dear enough for them.

June 17. I spent in cooking the turtle; I found in her threescore eggs, and her flesh was to me at that time the most savoury and pleasant that ever I tasted in my life, having had no flesh, but of goats and fowls, since I landed in this horrid place.

June 18. Rained all day, and stayed within. I thought at this time the rain felt cold, and I was something chilly, which I knew was not usual in that latitude.

June 19. Very ill, and shivering, as if the weather had been cold.

June 20. No rest all night, violent pains in my head, and feverish.

June 21. Very ill, frightened almost to death

with the apprehension of my sad condition, to be sick, and no help: prayed to God for the first time since the storm off of Hull, but scarce knew what I said, or why; my thoughts being all confused.

June 22. A little better, but under dreadful apprehensions of sickness.

June 23. Very bad again, cold shivering, and then a violent headache.

June 24. Much better.

June 25. An ague very violent; the fit held me seven hours, cold fit and hot, with faint sweats after it.

June 26. Better; and having no victuals to eat, took my gun, but found myself very weak; however, I killed a she-goat, and with much difficulty got it home, and broiled some of it and ate; I would fain have stewed it and made some broth, but had no pot.

June 27. The ague again so violent that I lay abed all day, and neither ate or drank. I was ready to perish for thirst, but so weak, I had no strength to stand up, or to get myself any water to drink: prayed to God again, but was light-headed, and when I was not, I was so ignorant that I knew not what to say; only I lay and cried, 'Lord look upon me, Lord pity me, Lord have mercy upon me.' I suppose I did nothing else for two or three hours, till the fit wearing off, I fell asleep, and did not wake till far in the night; when I waked, I found myself much refreshed, but weak, and exceeding thirsty. However, as I had no water in my whole habitation, I was forced to lie till morning, and went to sleep again. In this second sleep, I had this terrible dream.

I thought that I was sitting on the ground of the outside of my wall, and that I saw a man descend from a great black cloud, in a bright flame of fire, and light upon the ground. He was all over as bright as a flame, so that I could just bear to look towards him; his countenance was almost dreadful, impossible for words to describe; when he stepped upon the ground with his feet, I thought the earth trembled, and all the air looked, to my apprehension, as if it had been filled with flashes of fire.

He was no sooner landed upon the earth, but he moved forward towards me, with a long spear or weapon in his hand, to kill me; and when he came to a rising ground, at some distance, he spoke to me, or I heard a voice so terrible, that it is impossible to express the terror of it; all that I can say I understood, was this: 'Seeing all these things have not brought thee to repentance, now thou shalt die'; at which words, I thought he lifted up the spear that was in his hand, to kill me.

No one that shall ever read this account will expect that I should be able to describe the horrors of my soul at this terrible vision; nor is it any more possible to describe the impression that remained upon my mind when I awaked and found it was but a dream.

June 28. Having been somewhat refreshed with

the sleep I had had, and the fit being entirely off, I got up; and though the fright and terror of my dream was very great, yet I considered that the fit of the ague would return again the next day, and now was my time to get something to refresh and support myself when I should be ill; and the first thing I did, I filled a large square case bottle with water, and set it upon my table, in reach of my bed; and to take off the chill or aguish disposition of the water, I put about a quarter of a pint of rum into it, and mixed them together; then I got me a piece of the goat's flesh, and broiled it on the coals, but could eat very little; I walked about, but was very weak, and withal very sad and heavy-hearted in the sense of my miserable condition; dreading the return of my distemper the next day; at night I made my supper of three of the turtle's eggs, which I roasted in the ashes, and ate, as we call it, in the shell.

After I had eaten, I tried to walk, but found myself so weak that I could hardly carry the gun (for I never went out without that), so I went but a little way, and sat down upon the ground, look-ing out upon the sea, which was just before me, and very calm and smooth. As I sat here, some such thoughts as these occurred to me.

Why has God done this to me? What have I done to be thus used?

My conscience presently checked me in that inquiry, as if I had blasphemed, and methought it spoke to me like a voice: 'WRETCH! Dost thou ask what thou hast done? Look back upon a dreadful misspent life, and ask thyself what thou has *not* done; ask, Why is it that you wert not long ago destroyed? Why wert thou not drowned in Yarmouth? Killed in the fight when the ship was taken by the Sallee man-of-war? Devoured by the wild beasts on the coast of Africa? Or drowned *here*, when all the crew perished but thyself? Dost thou ask, "What have I done?"'

I was struck dumb with these reflections, as one astonished, and had not a word to say, no, not to answer to myself, but rose up pensive and sad, walked back to my retreat, and went up over my wall, as if I had been going to bed, but my thoughts were sadly disturbed, and I had no inclination to sleep; so I sat down in my chair and lighted my lamp, for it began to be dark. Now as the apprehension of the return of my distemper terrified me very much, it occurred to my thought, that the Brasilians take no medicine but their tobacco for almost all distempers; and I had a piece of a roll of tobacco in one of the chests which was quite cured, and some also that was green and not quite cured.

I went, directed by Heaven, no doubt; for in this chest I found a cure, both for soul and body. I opened the chest and found what I looked for, the tobacco; and as the few books I had saved lay there too, I took out one of the Bibles which I mentioned before, and which to this time I had not found leisure, or so much as inclination, to look into; I say, I took it out, and brought both that and the tobacco with me to the table.

What use to make of the tobacco I knew not, as to my distemper, or whether it was good for it or no; but I tried several experiments with it, as if I was resolved it should hit one way or other. I first took a piece of a leaf, and chewed it in my mouth, which indeed at first almost stupefied my brain, the tobacco being green and strong, and that I had not been much used to it; then I took some and steeped it an hour or two in some rum, and resolved to take a dose of it when I lay down; and lastly, I burnt some upon a pan of coals, and held my nose close over the smoke of it as long as I could bear it, as well for the heat as almost for suffocation.

In the interval of this operation, I took up the Bible and began to read, but my head was too much disturbed with the tobacco to bear reading, at least that time; only having opened the book casually, the first words that occurred to me were these: *Call on me in the day of trouble, and I will deliver, and thou shalt glorify me.*

It grew now late, and the tobacco had, as I said, dozed my head so much, that I inclined to sleep; so I left my lamp burning in the cave, lest I should want anything in the night, and went to bed; but before I lay down, I did what I never had done in all my life, I kneeled down and prayed to God to fulfil the promise to me, that if I called upon Him in the day of trouble, He would deliver me; after my broken and imperfect prayer was over, I drank the rum in which I had steeped the tobacco, which was so strong and rank from the tobacco, that I could scarce get it down; immediately upon this I went to bed. I found presently it flew up in my head violently, but I fell into a sound sleep, and waked no more till by the sun it must necessarily be near three o'clock in the afternoon the next day; nay, to this hour, I'm partly of the opinion that I slept all the next day and night, and till almost three that day after; for otherwise I knew not how I should lose a day out of my reckoning in the days of the week, as it appeared some years later I had done.

When I awaked I found myself exceedingly refreshed, and my spirits lively and cheerful; when I got up, I was stronger than I was the day before, and my stomach better, for I was hungry; and in short, I had no fit the next day, but continued much altered for the better; this was the 29th.

The 30th was my well day of course, and I went abroad with my gun, but did not care to travel too far. I killed a sea fowl or two, and brought them home, but was not very forward to eat them; so I ate some more of the turtle's eggs, which were very good. This evening I renewed the medicine which I had supposed did me good the day before, the tobacco steeped in rum, only I did not take so much as before, nor did I chew any of the leaf, or hold my head over the smoke; however I was not so well the next day, which was the first of July, as I hoped I should have been; for I had a touch of the cold fit, but it was not much.

July 2. I renewed the medicine all the three ways, and dosed myself with it as at first; and doubled the quantity which I drank.

July 3. I missed the fit for good and all, though I did not recover my full strength for some weeks after; while I was thus gathering strength, my thoughts ran exceedingly upon this scripture, *I will deliver thee*, and the impossibility of my deliverance lay much upon my mind.

July 4. In the morning I took the Bible, and beginning at the New Testament, I began seriously to read it, and imposed upon myself to read awhile every morning and every night, not tying myself to the number of chapters, but as long as my thoughts should engage me. It was not long after I set seriously to this work, but I found my heart more deeply and sincerely affected with the wickedness of my past life. The impression of my dream revived, and the words, *All these things have not brought thee to repentance*, ran seriously in my thought.

Now I began to construe the words mentioned above, *Call on me, and I will deliver you*, in a different sense from what I had ever done before; for then I had no notion of anything being called deliverance, but my being delivered from the captivity I was in; for though I was indeed at large in the place, yet the island was certainly a prison to me, and that in the worst sense in the world; but now I learned to take it in another sense. Now I looked back upon my past life with such horror, and my sins appeared so dreadful, that my soul sought nothing of God but deliverance from the load of guilt that bore down all my comfort: as for my solitary life, it was nothing; I did not so much as pray to be delivered from it, or think of it; it was all of no consideration in comparison to this.

My condition began now to be, though not less miserable as to my way of living, yet much easier to my mind; and my thoughts being directed, by a constant reading of the scripture and praying to God, to things of a higher nature, I had a great deal of comfort within, which till now I knew nothing of; also, as my health and strength returned, I bestirred myself to furnish myself with everything that I wanted, and make my way of living as regular as I could.

From the 4th of July to the 14th, I was chiefly employed in walking about with my gun in my hand, a little and a little at a time, as a man that was gathering up his strength after a fit of sickness; for it is hardly to be imagined how low I was, and to what weakness I was reduced. The application which I made use of was perfectly new, and perhaps what had never cured an ague before, neither can I recommend it to anyone and though it did carry off the fit, yet it rather contributed to weakening me; for I had frequent convulsions in my nerves and limbs for some time.

I learned from it also this in particular, that

being abroad in the rainy season was the most pernicious thing to my health that could be, especially in those rains which came attended with storms and hurricanes of wind; for as the rain which came in the dry season was always most accompanied with such storms, so I found that rain was much more dangerous than the rain which fell in September and October.

I had been now in this unhappy island above ten months; all possibility of deliverance from this condition seemed to be entirely taken from me; and I firmly believed that no human shape had ever set foot upon that place. Having now secured my habitation, as I thought, fully to my mind, I had a great desire to make a more perfect discovery of the island, and to see what other productions I might find, which I yet knew nothing of.

It was the 15th of July that I began to take a more particular survey of the island itself. I went up the creek first, where I had brought my rafts on shore; I found, after I came about two miles up, that the tide did not flow any higher, and that it was no more than a little brook of running water, and very fresh and good; but this being the dry season, there was hardly any water in some parts of it, at least not enough to run in any stream so as it could be perceived.

On the bank of this brook I found many pleasant meadows, plain, smooth, and covered with grass; and on the rising parts of them next to the higher grounds, where the water, as it might be supposed, never over-flowed, I found a great deal of tobacco, green, and growing to a great and very strong stalk; there were divers other plants which I had no notion of, or understanding about, and might perhaps have virtues of their own, which I could not find out.

The next day, the 16th, I went up the same way again, and after going somewhat farther than I had gone the day before, I found the brook, and the meadows began to cease, and the country became more woody than before; in this part I found different fruits, and particularly I found melons upon the ground in great abundance, and grapes upon the trees; the vines had spread indeed over the trees, and the clusters of grapes were just now in their prime, very ripe and rich. This was a surprising discovery, and I was exceeding glad of them; but I was warned by my experience to eat sparingly of them, remembering that when I was ashore in Barbary, the eating of grapes killed several of our English men who were slaves there, by throwing them into fluxes and fevers. But I found an excellent use for these grapes, and that was to cure or dry them in the sun, and keep them as dried grapes or raisins are kept, which I thought would be, as indeed they were, as wholesome as agreeable to eat, when no grapes might be had.

I spent all that evening there, and went not back to my habitation, which, by the way, was the first night, as I might say, I had lain from home. In the night I took my first contrivance, and got up into a tree, where I slept well, and the next morning proceeded upon my discovery, travelling near four miles, as I might judge by the length of the valley, keeping still due north, with a ridge of hills on the south and north-side of me.

At the end of this march I came to an opening, where the country seemed to descend to the west, and a little spring of fresh water, which issued out of the side of the hill by me, ran the other way, that is, due east; and the country appeared so fresh, so green, so flourishing, everything being in a constant verdure or flourish of spring, that it looked like a planted garden.

I descended a little on the side of that delicious vale, surveying it with a secret kind of pleasure (though mixed with my other afflicting thoughts) to think that this was all my own, that I was king and lord of all this country indefeasibly, and had a right of possession; and if I could convey it, I might have it in inheritance as completely as any lord of a manor in England. I saw here abundance of cocoa trees, orange, and lemon, and citron trees; but all wild, and very few bearing any fruit, at least not then. However, the green limes that I gathered were not only pleasant to eat, but very wholesome; and I mixed their juice afterwards with water, which made it very wholesome, and very cool and refreshing.

I found now I had business enough to gather and carry home; and I resolved to lay up a store, as well of grapes as limes and lemons, to furnish myself for the wet season, which I knew was approaching.

I therefore gathered a great heap of grapes in one place, and a lesser heap in another place, and a great parcel of limes and lemons in another place; and taking a few of each with me, I travelled homeward, and resolved to come again, and bring a bag or sack, or what I could make, to carry the rest home.

Accordingly, having spent three days in this journey, I came home; so I must now call my tent and my cave. But, before I got thither, the grapes were spoiled; the richness of the fruits and the weight of the juice having broken them and bruised them, they were good for little or nothing; as to the limes, they were good, but I could bring but a few.

The next day, being the 19th, I went back, having made me two small bags to bring home my harvest; but I was surprised, when coming to my heap of grapes, which were so rich and fine when I gathered them, I found them all spread about, trod to pieces, and dragged about, some here, some there, and many eaten and devoured. By this I concluded there were some wild creatures thereabouts which had done this; but what they were I knew not.

However, as I found that there was no laying them up in heaps, and no carrying them away in a sack, but that one way they would be destroyed, and the other way they would be crushed with their own weight, I took another course; for I gathered a large quantity of the grapes, and hung them up upon the out branches of the trees, that they might cure and dry in the sun; and as for the limes and lemons, I carried as many back as I could well stand under.

When I came home from this journey, I contemplated with great pleasure the fruitfulness of that valley and the pleasantness of the situation, the security from storms on that side of the water, and the wood, and concluded that I had pitched upon a place to fix my abode, which was by far the worst part of the country. Upon the whole I began to consider removing my habitation; and to look out for a place equally safe as where I now was, situated, if possible, in that pleasant, fruitful part of the island.

This thought ran long in my head, and I was exceeding fond of it for some time, the pleasantness of the place tempting me; but when I came to a nearer view of it, and to consider that I was now by the sea-side, where it was at least possible that something might happen to my advantage, and by the same ill fate that brought me hither, might bring some other unhappy wretches to the same place; and though it was scarce probable that any such thing should ever happen, yet to enclose myself among the hills and woods, in the centre of the island, was to anticipate my bondage, and to render such an affair not only improbable, but impossible; and that therefore I ought not by any means to remove.

However, I was so enamoured of this place, that I spent much of my time there for the whole remaining part of the month of July; and though upon second thoughts I resolved as above, not to remove, yet I built me a little kind of a bower, and surrounded it at a distance with a strong fence, being a double hedge, as high as I could reach, well staked, and filled between with brush-wood; and here I lay very secure, sometimes two or three nights together, always going over it with a ladder, as before; so that I fancied now I had my country house, and my sea-coast house: and this work took me up to the beginning of August.

1 had but newly finished my fence, and began to enjoy my labour, but the rains came on, and made me stick close to my first habitation; for though I had made me a tent like the other, with a piece of a sail, and spread it very well, yet I had not the shelter of a hill to keep me from storms, nor a cave behind me to retreat into, when the rains were extraordinary.

About the beginning of August, as I said, I had finished my bower, and began to enjoy myself. The third of August, I found the grapes I had hung up were perfectly dried, and indeed were excellent good raisins, so I began to take them down from the trees, and it was very happy that I did so; for the rains which followed would have spoiled them, and I had lost the best part of my winter food; for I had above two hundred large bunches of them. No sooner had I taken them all down, and carried most of them home to my cave, but it began to rain, and from hence, which was the fourteenth of August, it rained more or less, every day, till the middle of October; and sometimes so violently that I could not stir out of my cave for several days.

In this confinement I began to be straitened for food, but venturing out twice, I one day killed a goat, and the last day, which was the twenty-sixth, found a very large tortoise, which was a treat to me, and my food was regulated thus: I ate a bunch of raisins for my breakfast, a piece of the goat's flesh or of the turtle for my dinner, broiled; for, to my great misfortune, I had no vessel to boil or stew anything; and two or three of the turtle's eggs for my supper.

During this confinement in my cover by the rain, I worked daily two or three hours at enlarging my cave, and by degrees worked it on towards one side, till I came to the outside of the hill, and made a door or way out, which came beyond my fence or wall, and so I came in and out this way; but I was not perfectly easy at lying so open; for as I had managed myself before, I was in a perfect enclosure, whereas now I thought I lay exposed, and open for anything to come in upon me; and yet I could not perceive that there was any living thing to fear, the biggest creature that I had yet seen upon the island being a goat.

September the thirtieth. I was now come to the unhappy anniversary of my landing. I cast up the notches on my post, and found I had been on shore three hundred and sixty-five days. I kept this day as a solemn fast, setting it apart to religious exercise.

## 6

A little after this my ink began to fail me, and so I contented myself to use it more sparingly, and to write down only the most remarkable events of my life, without continuing a daily memorandum of other things.

I made a little discovery which was of use to me afterwards. As soon as the rains were over, and the weather began to settle, which was about the month of November, I made a visit up the country to my bower, where though I had not been some months, yet I found all things just as I left them. The circle or double hedge that I had made was not only firm and entire, but the stakes which I had cut out of some trees that grew thereabouts were all shot out and grown with long branches, as much as a willow-tree usually shoots the first year after lopping its head. I could not tell what tree to call it, that these stakes were cut from. I was surprised, and yet very well pleased, to see the young trees grow; and I pruned them, and led them up to grow as much alike as I could; and it is scarce credible how beautiful a figure they grew into in three years; so that though the hedge made a circle of about twenty-five yards in diameter, yet the trees, for such I might now call them, soon covered it; and it was a complete shade, sufficient to lodge under all the dry season.

This made me resolve to cut some more stakes, and make me a hedge like this in a semicircle round my wall; I mean that of my first dwelling, which I did; and placing the trees or stakes in a double row, at about eight yards' distance from my first fence, they grew presently, and were at first a fine cover to my habitation, and afterwards served for a defence also, as I shall observe in its order.

When it rained, I found much employment (and very suitable also to the time), for there were many things which I had no way to furnish myself with, but by hard labour and constant application; particularly, I tried many ways to make myself a basket, but all the twigs I could get for the purpose proved so brittle that they would do nothing. It proved of excellent advantage to me now, that when I was a boy, I used to take great delight in standing at a basket-makers' in the town where my father lived, to see them make their wicker-ware; and being, as boys usually are, very officious to help, and a great observer of the manner how they worked those things, and sometimes lending a hand, I had by this means full knowledge of the methods of it, so that I wanted nothing but the materials; when it came into my mind that the twigs of that tree from whence I cut my stakes that grew, might possibly be as tough as the sallows and willows and osiers in England, and I resolved to try.

Accordingly the next day, I went to my country house, as I called it, and cutting some of the smaller twigs, I found them to my purpose as much as I could desire; whereupon I came the next time prepared with a hatchet to cut down a quantity, which I soon found, for there was great plenty of them; these I set up to dry within my circle or hedge, and when they were fit for use, I carried them to my cave, and here during the next season, I employed myself in making, as well as I could, a great many baskets, both to carry earth, or to carry or lay up anything as I had occasion; and though I did not finish them very handsomely, yet I made them sufficiently serviceable for my purpose; and thus afterwards I took care never to be without them; and as my wicker-ware decayed, I made more; especially I made strong deep baskets to place my corn in, instead of sacks, when I should come to have any quantity of it.

Having mastered the difficulty, and employed a world of time about it, I bestirred myself to see if possible how to supply two wants. I had no vessels to hold anything that was liquid, except two runlets which were almost full of rum, and some glass bottles, some of the common size, and others which were case bottles, square, for the holding of waters, spirits, etc. I had not so much as a pot to boil anything, except a great kettle, which I saved out of the ship, and which was too big for such use as I desired it, to make broth and stew a bit of meat by itself. The second thing I would fain have had, was a tobacco-pipe, but it was impossible to make one.

I employed myself in planting my second rows of stakes, and in this wicker-working, all the summer or dry season, when another business took me up more time than it could be imagined I could spare.

I mentioned before that I had a great mind to see the whole island, and that I had travelled up the brook, and so on to where I built my bower, and where I had an opening quite to the sea on the other side of the island. I now resolved to travel quite cross to the sea-shore on that side; so taking my gun, a hatchet, and a larger quantity of powder and shot than usual, with two biscuit cakes and a great bunch of raisins in my pouch for my store, I began my journey. When I had passed the vale where my bower stood, I came within view of the sea, to the west, and it being a very clear day, I fairly descried land, whether an island or a continent, I could not tell; but it lay very high, extending from the west to the WSW at a very great distance; by my guess it could not be less than fifteen or twenty leagues off.

I could not tell what part of the world this might be, otherwise than that I knew it must be part of America, and, as I concluded by all my observations, must be near the Spanish dominions, and perhaps was all inhabited by savages, where if I should have landed, I had been in a worse condition than I was now; and therefore I acquiesced in the dispositions of Providence, which I began now to own and to believe ordered everything for the best; I say, I quieted my mind with this, and left afflicting myself with fruitless wishes of being there.

Besides, after some pause upon this affair, I considered that if this land was the Spanish coast, I should certainly, one time or other, see some vessel pass or repass one way or other; but if not, then it was the savage coast between the Spanish country and Brasils, which are indeed the worst of savages; for they are cannibals, or men-eaters, and fail not to murder and devour all the human bodies that fall into their hands.

With these considerations I walked leisurely forward; I found that side of the island where I now was much pleasanter than mine, the open or savanna fields sweet, adorned with flowers and grass, and full of very fine woods. I saw abundance of parrots, and fain I would have caught one, if possible, to have kept it to be tame, and taught it to speak to me. I did, after some pains taking, catch a young parrot, for I knocked it down with a stick, and having recovered it, I brought it home; but it was some years before I could make him speak: however, at last I taught him to call me by my name very familiarly.

I was exceedingly diverted with this journey. I

found in the low grounds hares, as I thought them to be, and foxes, but they differed greatly from all the other kinds I had met with; nor could I satisfy myself to eat them, though I killed several. But I had no want of food, and of that which was very good too; especially goats, pigeons, turtle or tortoise, and grapes.

I never travelled in this journey above two miles outright in a day, or thereabouts; but I took so many turns and returns to see what discoveries I could make, that I came weary enough to the place where I resolved to spend the night; and then I either reposed myself in a tree, or surrounded myself with a row of stakes set upright in the ground, either from one tree to another, or so as no wild creature could come at me without waking me.

As soon as I came to the sea-shore, I was surprised to see that I had taken up my lot on the worst side of the island; for here the shore was covered with innumerable turtles, where on the other side I had found but three in a year and half. Here was also an infinite number of fowls of many kinds, some which I had seen and some which I had not seen before, and many of them very good meat; but such as I knew not the names of, except those called penguins.

I could have shot as many as I pleased, but was very sparing of my powder and shot: and therefore had more mind to kill a she-goat, if I could, which I could better feed on; and though there were many goats here more than on my side of the island, yet it was with much more difficulty that I could come near them, the country being flat and even, and they saw me much sooner than when I was on the hill.

I confess this side of the country was much pleasanter than mine, but yet I had not the least inclination to remove; for as I was fixed in my habitation, it became natural to me, and I seemed all the while I was here to be as it were upon a journey, and from home. However, I travelled along the shore of the sea towards the east, I suppose about twelve miles; and then setting up a great pole upon the shore for a mark, I concluded I would go home again; and that the next journey I took should be on the other side of the island, east from my dwelling, and so round till I came to my post again.

I took another way to come back than that I went, thinking I could easily keep all the island so much in my view that I could not miss finding my first dwelling by viewing the country; but I found myself mistaken; for being come about two or three miles, I found myself descended into a very large valley; but so surrounded with hills, and those hills covered with wood, that I could not see which was my way by any direction but that of the sun, nor even then, unless I knew very well the position of the sun at that time of the day.

It happened to my farther misfortune, that the weather proved hazy for three or four days while

I was in this valley; and not being able to see the sun, I wandered about very uncomfortably, and at last was obliged to find out the sea-side, look for my post, and come back the same way I went; and then by easy journeys I turned homeward, the weather being exceeding hot, and my gun, ammunition, hatchet, and other things very heavy.

In this journey I surprised a young kid, and saved it alive. I had a great mind to bring it home if I could; for I had often been musing whether it might not be possible to get a kid or two, and so raise a breed of tame goats, which might supply me when my powder and shot should be all spent.

I made a collar to this little creature, and with a string which I made of some rope-yarn, which I always carried about me, I led him along, though with some difficulty, till I came to my bower, and there I enclosed him and left him; for I was very impatient to be at home, from whence I had been absent above a month.

I cannot express what a satisfaction it was to me, to come into my old hutch, and lie down in my hammock-bed. This little wandering journey, without settled place of abode, had been so unpleasant to me, that my own house, as I called it to myself, was a perfect settlement to me, compared to that; and it rendered everything about me so comfortable, that I resolved I would never go a great way from it again, while it should be my lot to stay on the island.

I reposed myself here a week, to rest after my

long journey; during which, most of the time was taken up in the weighty affair of making a cage for my Poll, who began now to be thoroughly domesticated and to be mighty well acquainted with me. Then I began to think of the poor kid, which I had penned in within my little circle, and resolved to go and fetch it home, or give it some food; accordingly I went, and found it where I left it, for indeed it could not get out, but almost starved for want of food. I went and cut boughs of trees, and branches of such shrubs as I could find, and threw it over, and having fed it, I tied it as I did before, to lead it away; but it was so tame with being hungry, that I had no need to have tied it; for it followed me like a dog; and as I continually fed it, the creature became so loving, so gentle, and so fond, that it would never leave me afterwards.

The rainy season of the autumnal equinox was now come, and I kept the 30th of September in the same solemn manner as before, being the anniversary of my landing on the island, having now been there two years, and no more prospect of being delivered than the first day I came there.

It was now that I began sensibly to feel how much more happy this life I now led was, with all its miserable circumstances, than the wicked, cursed, abominable life I led all the past part of my days; and now I changed both my sorrows and my joys; my very desires altered, and my delights were perfectly new from what they were at my first coming, or indeed for the two years past.

Before, as I walked about, either on my hunting, or for viewing the country, the anguish of my soul at my condition would break out upon me on a sudden, and my very heart would die within me, to think of the woods, the mountains, the deserts I was in; and how I was a prisoner, locked up with the eternal bars and bolts of the ocean, in an uninhabited wilderness, without redemption. In the midst of the greatest composures of my mind, this would break out upon me like a storm, and make me wring my hands, and weep like a child. Sometimes it would take me in the middle of my work, and I would immediately sit down and sigh, and look upon the ground for an hour or two together; and this was still worse to me; for if I could burst out into tears, or vent myself by words, it would go off, and the grief having exhausted itself would abate.

But now I began to conclude in my mind that it was possible for me to be more happy in this forsaken, solitary condition than it was probable I should ever have been in any other particular state in the world; and with this thought I gave thanks to God for bringing me to this place.

Thus, and in this disposition of mind, I began my third year; and though I have not given the reader the trouble of so particular an account of my works this year as the first, yet in general it may be observed that I was very seldom idle; but having regularly divided my time, according to the several daily employments that were before me, such as, first, my duty to God, and the reading of the scriptures, which I constantly set apart some time for thrice every day; secondly, the going abroad with my gun for food, which generally took up three hours in every morning, when it did not rain; thirdly, the ordering, curing, preserving, and cooking what I had killed or caught for my supply; these took up a great part of the day; also it is to be considered that in the middle of the day, when the sun was in the zenith, the violence of the heat was too great to stir out; so that about four hours in the evening was all the time I could be supposed to work in; with this exception, that sometimes I changed my hours of hunting and working, and went to work in the morning, and abroad with my gun in the afternoon.

To this short time allowed for labour, I desire may be added the exceeding laboriousness of my work; the many hours which, for want of tools, want of help, and want of skill, everything I did took up out of my time. For example, I was full two and forty days making me a board for a long shelf, which I wanted in my cave; whereas two sawyers, with their tools and a sawpit, would have cut six of them out of the same tree in half a day.

Likewise, caring for my corn took a great deal of time; for I had to contrive ways of preventing both beasts and fowl from eating it. For the beasts, I surrounded my arable land with a hedge; for the fowl, I discovered that if I shot some and hung them up for a scarecrow, the other birds would not come near.

Then, I had no plough to turn up the earth, no spade or shovel to dig it. Well, this I conquered, by making a wooden spade, as I observed before; but this did my work in but a wooden manner, and though it cost me a great many days to make it, yet for want of iron it not only wore out the sooner, but made my work the harder, and made it be performed much worse.

However, this I bore with, and was content to work it out with patience, and bear with the badness of performance. When the corn was sown, I had no harrow, but was forced to go over it myself and drag a great heavy bough of a tree over it, to scratch it, as it may be called, rather than rake or harrow it.

When it was growing and grown, there were many things I wanted, to fence it, secure it, mow or reap it, cure and carry it home, thrash, part it from the chaff, and save it. Then I wanted a mill to grind it, sieve to dress it, yeast and salt to make it into bread, and an oven to bake it, and yet all these things I did without, as shall be observed; and yet the corn was an inestimable comfort and advantage to me too. All this, as I said, made everything laborious and tedious to me, but that there was no help for; neither was my time so much loss to me, because, as I had divided it, a certain part of it was every day appointed to these works; and as I resolved to use none of the corn for bread till I had a greater quantity by me; I had the next six months to apply myself wholly by labour and invention to furnish myself with utensils proper for performing all the operations necessary for making the corn (when I had it) fit for my use.

Thus I discovered, after many miserable failures, how to make pots and plates out of clay; and how to fire them until they could serve as cooking utensils. I made myself a pestle and mortar out of the same iron-wood with which I had fashioned my spade. My next difficulty was to make a sieve, and here I was at a loss, until I remembered I had among the clothes which were saved out of the ship, some neck-cloths of callicoe or muslin; and with some pieces of these I made three small sieves, but proper enough for the work.

The baking part was the next thing to be considered, and how I should make bread when I came to have corn; for first I had no yeast; as to that part, as there was no supplying the want, so I did not concern myself much about it; but for an oven, I was indeed in great pain. At length I found out an experiment for that also, which was this: I made some earthen vessels, very broad, but not deep; that is to say, about two foot in diameter, and not above nine inches deep; these I burnt in the fire, as I had done the others, and laid them by; and when I wanted to bake, I made a great fire upon my hearth, which I had paved with some square tiles of my own making and burning also; but I should not call them square.

When the fire-wood was burnt pretty much into embers, or live coals, I drew them forward upon this hearth so as to cover it all over, and there I let them lie till the hearth was very hot; then sweeping away all the embers, I set down my loaf or loaves, and turning the earthen pot upside down upon them, drew the embers all round the outside of the pot, to keep in, and add to the heat; and thus, as well as in the best oven in the world, I baked my barley loaves, and became in little time a complete pastry-cook into the bargain; for I made myself several cakes of the rice, and puddings; indeed I made no pies, neither had I anything to put into them, supposing I had, except the flesh either of fowls or goats.

It need not be wondered at, if all these things took me up most part of the third year of my abode here; for it is to be observed that in the intervals of these things, I had my new harvest and husbandry to manage; for I reaped my corn in its season, and carried it home as well as I could, and laid it up in the ear in my large baskets, till I had time to rub it out; for I had no floor to thrash it on, or instruments to thrash it with.

And now indeed, my stock of corn increasing, I really wanted to build my barns bigger. I wanted a place to lay it up in; for the increase of the corn now yielded me so much, that I had of the barley about twenty bushels, and of the rice as much, or more; insomuch that now I resolved to begin to use it freely; for my bread had been quite gone a great while; also I resolved to see what quantity would be sufficient for me a whole year, and to sow but once a year.

Upon the whole, I found that the forty bushels of barley and rice was much more than I could consume in a year; so I resolved to sow just the same quantity every year that I sowed the last, in hopes that such a quantity would fully provide me with bread etc.

All the while these things were doing, you may be sure my thoughts ran many times upon the prospect of land which I had seen from the other side of the island, and I was not without secret wishes that I were on shore there, fancying seeing the mainland, and in an inhabited country I might find some way or other to convey myself farther, and perhaps at last find some means of escape.

But all this while I made no allowance for the dangers of such a condition, and how I might fall into the hands of savages, and perhaps such as I might have reason to think far worse than the lions and tigers of Africa; that if I once came into their power, I should run a hazard more than a thousand to one of being killed, and perhaps of being eaten; for I had heard that the people of the Carribean coast were cannibals, or man-eaters; and I knew by the latitude that I could not be far off from that shore. Even supposing they were not

cannibals, yet they might kill me, as many Europe-
ans who had fallen into their hands had been
served, even when they had been ten or twenty
together; much more I that was but one, and
could make little or no defence. All these things, I
say, which I ought to have considered well, and
did cast up in my thoughts afterwards, yet took
up none of my apprehensions at first; but my
head run mightily upon the thought of getting
over to the shore.

Then I thought I would go and look at our
ship's boat, which, as I have said, was blown up
upon the shore, a great way in the storm, when we
were first cast away. She lay almost where she did
at first, but not quite; and was turned by the force
of the waves and the winds almost bottom up-
wards, against a high ridge of beachy rough sand;
but no water about her as before.

If I had had hands to have refitted her, and to
have launched her into the water, the boat would
have done well enough, and I might have gone
back into the Brasils with her easily enough; but I
might have foreseen that I could no more turn her
and set her upright upon her bottoms, than I
could remove the island. However, I went to the
woods, and cut levers and rollers, and brought
them to the boat, resolved to try what I could do,
suggesting to myself that if I could but turn her
down, I might easily repair the damage she had
received, and she would be a very good boat, and
I might go to sea in her very easily.

I spared no pains, indeed, in this piece of fruitless toil, and spent, I think, three or four weeks
about it; at last, finding it impossible to heave it
up with my little strength, I fell to digging away
the sand, to undermine it, and so to make it fall
down, setting pieces of wood to thrust and guide
it right in the fall.

But when I had done this, I was unable to stir it
up again, or to get under it, much less to move it
forward towards the water; so I was forced to give
it over; and yet, though I gave over the hopes of
the boat, my desire to venture over for the main
increased, rather than decreased, as the means for
it seemed impossible.

In the middle of this work, I finished my fourth
year in this place, and kept my anniversary with
the same devotion, and with as much comfort as
ever before. I had now brought my state of life to
be much easier in itself than it was at first, and
much easier to my mind, as well as to my body. I
frequently sat down to my meat with thankfulness,
and admired the hand of God's providence, which
had thus spread my table in the wilderness. I
learned to look more upon the bright side of my
condition, and less upon the dark side, and to
consider what I enjoyed, rather than what I
wanted; and this gave me sometimes such secret
comforts, that I cannot express them; and which I
take notice of here, to put those discontented
people in mind of it, who cannot enjoy comfortably what God has given them; because they see

and covet something that He has not given them. All our discontents about what we want appeared to me to spring from the want of thankfulness for what we have.

I had now been here so long that many things which I brought on shore for my help were either quite gone or very much wasted and near spent.

My ink, as I observed, had been gone some time, all but a very little, which I eked out with water a little and a little, till it was so pale it scarce left any appearance of black upon the paper. As long as it lasted, I made use of it to minute down the days of the month on which any remarkable thing happened to me.

The next thing to my ink's being wasted, was that of my bread, I mean the biscuit which I brought out of the ship; this I had husbanded to the last degree, allowing myself but one cake of bread a day for above a year, and yet I was quite without bread for near a year before I got any corn of my own, and great reason I had to be thankful that I had any at all, the getting it being, as has been already observed, next to miraculous.

My clothes began to decay too, mightily: I saved the skins of all the creatures that I killed, I mean four-footed ones, and I hung them up stretched out with sticks in the sun, by which means some of them were so dry and hard that they were fit for little, but others, it seems, were very useful. The first thing I made of these was a great cap for my head, with the hair on the outside to shoot off the rain; and this I performed so well, that after this I made me a suit of clothes wholly of these skins, that is to say, a waistcoat, and breeches open at knees, and both loose, for they were rather wanting to keep me cool than to keep me warm. I must not omit to acknowledge that they were wretchedly made; for if I was a bad carpenter, I was a worse tailor. However, they were such as I made very good shift with; and when I was abroad, if it happened to rain, the hair of my waistcoat and cap being outermost, I was kept very dry.

After this I spent a great deal of time and pains to make me an umbrella; I was indeed in great want of one, and had a great mind to make one; I had seen them made in the Brasils, where they are very useful in the great heats which are there; and I felt the heats every jot as great here, and greater too, being nearer the equator; besides, as I was obliged to be much abroad, it was a most useful thing to me, as well for the rains as the heats. I took a world of pains at it, and was a great while before I could make anything likely to hold; nay, after I thought I had hit the way, I spoiled two or three before I made one to my mind; but at last I made one that answered indifferently well. The main difficulty I found was to make it to let down. I could make it to spread, but if it did not let down too, and draw in, it was not portable for me any way but just over my head, which would not do. However, at last, as I said, I made one to

answer, and covered it with skins, the hair up-
wards, so that it cast off the rains, and kept off the
sun so effectually that I could walk out in the
hottest of the weather with greater advantage than
I could before in the coolest, and when I had no
need of it, could close it and carry it under my
arm.

Thus I lived mighty comfortably, my mind
being entirely composed by resigning to the will
of God, and throwing myself wholly upon the
disposal of His providence. This made my life
better than sociable, for when I began to regret
the want of conversation, I would ask myself
whether thus conversing mutually with my own
thoughts, and, as I hope I may say, with even
God Himself, was not better than the utmost
enjoyment of human society in the world.

## 7

I cannot say that after this, for five years, any extraordinary thing happened to me, but I lived on in the same course, in the same posture and place, just as before; the chief things I was employed in, besides my yearly labour of planting my barley and rice, and curing my raisins, of both which I always kept up just enough to have sufficient stock of one year's provisions beforehand; I say, besides this yearly labour, and my daily labour of going out with my gun, I had one labour, to make me a canoe, and though I was near two years about it, yet I never grudged my labour, in hopes of having a boat to go off to sea at last.

However, though my little canoe was finished, yet the size of it was not at all answerable to the design which I had in view of venturing over to the terra firma, where it was above forty miles broad; accordingly, the smallness of my boat assisted to put an end to that design, and now I thought no more of it: but as I had a boat, my next design was to make a tour round the island; for as I had been on the other side in one place, crossing, as I have already described it, over the land, so the discoveries I made in that little journey made me very eager to see other parts of the coast; and now I had a boat, I thought of nothing but sailing round the island.

For this purpose, that I might do everything with discretion and consideration, I fitted up a little mast to my boat, and made a sail to it out of some of the pieces of the ship's sail, which lay in store, and of which I had a great stock by me.

Having fitted my mast and sail, and tried the boat, I found she would sail very well. Then I made little lockers, or boxes, at either end of my boat, to put provisions, necessaries, and ammunitions into, to be kept dry, either from rain or the spray of the sea; and a little long hollow place I cut in the inside of the boat, where I could lay my gun, making a flap to hang down over it to keep it dry.

I fixed my umbrella also in a step at the stern, like a mast, to stand over my head, and keep the heat of the sun off me like an awning; and thus I every now and then took a little voyage upon the sea, but never went far out, nor far from the little creek; but at last, being eager to view the circumference of my little kingdom, I resolved upon my tour, and accordingly I victualled my ship for the voyage, putting in two dozen of my loaves (cakes I should rather call them) or barley bread, an earthen pot full of parched rice, a food I ate a great deal of, a little bottle of rum, half a goat, and powder and shot for killing more.

It was the sixth of November, in the sixth year of my reign, or my captivity, which you please, that I set out on this voyage, and I found it much longer than I expected; for though the island itself was not very large, yet when I came to the east side of it, I found a great ledge of rocks stretching above two leagues into the sea, some above water, some under it; and beyond that, a shoal of sand, lying dry half a league more; so that I was obliged to go a great way out to sea to double the point.

When first I discovered them, I was going to give over my enterprise, and come back again, not knowing how far it might oblige me to go out to sea; and above all, doubting how I should get back again; so I came to anchor; for I had made me a kind of an anchor with a piece of a broken grapnel which I got out of the ship.

Having secured my boat, I took my gun and went on shore, climbing up upon a hill which seemed to overlook that point, where I saw the full extent of it, and resolved to venture.

In my viewing the sea from that hill where I stood, I perceived a strong, and indeed a most furious current, which ran to the east, and even came close to the point; and I took the more notice of it, because I saw there might be some danger; that when I came into it, I might be carried out to sea by the strength of it, and not be able to make the island again; and indeed, had I not first gone up this hill, I believe it would have been so; for there was the same current on the

other side the island, only that it set off at a
farther distance; and I saw there was a strong
eddy under the shore; so I had nothing to do but
to get in out of the first current, and I should
presently be in an eddy.

I lay here, however, two days; because the wind
blowing pretty fresh at ESE, and that being just
contrary to the said current, made a great breaking
of the sea upon the point; so that it was not safe
for me to keep too close to the shore for the
breakers, nor to go too far off because of the
stream.

The third day in the morning, the wind having
abated overnight, the sea was calm, and I ventured; but I am a warning again to all rash and
ignorant pilots; for no sooner was I come to the
point, when even I was not my boat's length from
the shore, but I found myself in a great depth of
water, and a current like the sluice of a mill: it
carried my boat along with it with such violence
that all I could do could not keep her so much as
on the edge of it; but I found it hurried me farther
and farther out from the eddy, which was on my
left hand. There was no wind stirring to help me,
and all I could do with my paddles signified
nothing, and now I began to give myself over for
lost; for as the current was on both sides the
island, I knew in a few leagues distance they must
join again, and then I was irrecoverably gone; nor
did I see any possibility of avoiding it; so that I
had no prospect before me but of perishing, not

by the sea, for that was calm enough, but of
starving for hunger. I had indeed found a tortoise
on the shore, as big almost as I could lift, and had
tossed it into the boat; and I had a great jar of
fresh water, that is to say, one of my earthen pots;
but what was all this to being driven into the vast
ocean, where, to be sure, there was no shore, no
mainland or island, for a thousand leagues at
least?

It is scarce possible to imagine the consternation
I was now in, being driven from my beloved
island (for so it appeared to me now to be) into
the wide ocean, almost two leagues, and in the
utmost despair of ever recovering it again. However, I worked hard, till indeed my strength was
almost exhausted, and kept my boat as much to
the northward, that is, towards the side of the
current which the eddy lay on, as possibly I could;
when about noon, as the sun passed the meridian,
I thought I felt a little breeze of wind in my face,
springing up from the SSE. This cheered my
heart a little, and especially when in about half an
hour more it blew a pretty small gentle gale. By
this time I was a frightful distance from the island,
and had the least cloud of hazy weather intervened, I had been undone another way too; for I
had no compass on board, and should never have
known how to have steered towards the island, if
I had but once lost sight of it; but the weather
continuing clear, I applied myself to get up my
mast again, and spread my sail, standing away to

the north as much as possible, to get out of the current.

Just as I had set my mast and sail, and the boat began to stretch away, I saw even by the clearness of the water some alteration of the current was near; for where the current was so strong, the water was foul; but perceiving the water clear, I found the current abate, and presently I found to the east, at about half a mile, a breaking of the sea upon some rocks; these rocks I found caused the current to part again, and as the main stress of it ran away more southerly, leaving the rocks to the north-east, so the other returned by the repulse of the rocks, and made a strong eddy, which ran back again to the north-west, with a very sharp stream.

They who know what it is to have a reprieve brought to them upon the scaffold, or to be rescued from thieves just about to murder them, or who have been in suchlike extremities, may guess what my present joy was, and how gladly I put my boat into the stream of this eddy, and the wind also freshening, how gladly I spread my sail to it, running cheerfully before the wind, and with a strong tide or eddy underfoot.

This eddy carried me about a league in my way back again directly towards the island, but about two leagues more to the northward than the current which carried me away at first; so that when I came near the island, I found myself open to the northern shore of it, that is to say, the other end of the island opposite to that which I went out from.

When I had made something more than a league of way by the help of this current or eddy, I found it was spent and served me no farther. However, I found that being between the two great currents, that on the south side which had hurried me away, and that on the north which lay about a league on the other side; I say, between these two, in the wake of the island, I found the water at least still and running no way, and having still a breeze of wind fair for me, I kept on steering directly for the island, though not making such fresh way as I did before.

About four o'clock in the evening, being then within about a league of the island, I found the point of the rocks which occasioned this disaster, stretching out as is described before to the southward, and casting off the current more southwardly, had of course made another eddy to the north, and this I found very strong, but not directly setting the way my course lay, which was due west, but almost full north. However, having a fresh wind, I stretched across this eddy slanting north-west, and in about an hour came within about a mile of the shore, where it being smooth water, I soon got to land.

When I was on shore I fell on my knees and gave God thanks for my deliverance, resolving to lay aside all thoughts of my deliverance by my boat; and refreshing myself with such things as I had, I brought my boat close to the shore in a little cove that I had spied under some trees, and lay down to sleep, being quite spent with the labour and fatigue of the voyage.

I was now at a great loss which way to get home with my boat. I had run so much hazard, and knew too much, to think of attempting it by the way I went out, and what might be at the other side (I mean the west side) I knew not, nor had I any mind to run any more ventures; so I only resolved in the morning to make my way westward along the shore and to see if there was no creek where I might lay up my frigate in safety, so as to have her again if I wanted her; in about three mile or thereabout, coasting the shore, I came to a very good inlet or bay about a mile over, which narrowed till it came to a very little rivulet or brook, where I found a very convenient harbour for my boat, and where she lay as if she had been in a little dock made on purpose for her. Here I put in, and having stowed my boat very safe, I went on shore to look about me and see where I was.

I soon found I had but a little passed by the place where I had been before, when I travelled on foot to that shore; so taking nothing out of my boat but my gun and my umbrella, for it was exceeding hot, I began my march. The way was comfortable enough after such a voyage as I had been upon, and I reached my old bower in the evening, where I found everything standing as I left it; for I always kept it in good order, being, as I said before, my country house.

I got over the fence, and laid me down in the shade to rest my limbs, for I was very weary, and fell asleep. But judge you, if you can, that read my story, what a surprise I must be in, when I was waked out of my sleep by a voice calling me by my name several times, 'Robin, Robin, Robin Crusoe, poor Robin Crusoe, where are you, Robin Crusoe? Where are you? Where have you been?'

I was so dead asleep at first, being fatigued with rowing the first part of the day, and with walking the latter part, that I did not wake thoroughly, but dozing between sleeping and waking, thought I dreamed that somebody spoke to me: but as the voice continued to repeat 'Robin Crusoe, Robin Crusoe', at last I began to wake more perfectly, and was at first dreadfully frightened, and started up in the utmost consternation. But no sooner were my eyes open, than I saw my Poll sitting on the top of the hedge, and immediately knew that it was he that spoke to me; for just in such bemoaning language I had used to talk to him and teach him; and he had learned it so perfectly, that he would sit upon my finger, and lay his bill close to my face, and cry, 'Poor Robin Crusoe, where are you? Where have you been? How come you here?' and such things as I had taught him.

However, even though I knew it was the parrot, and that indeed it could be nobody else, it was a good while before I could compose myself. First, I was amazed how the creature got thither, and then, how he should just keep about the place, and nowhere else: but as I was well satisfied it could be nobody but honest Poll, I got over it; and holding out my hand, and calling him by his name, Poll, the sociable creature came to me, and sat upon my thumb, as he used to do, and continued talking to me, 'Poor Robin Crusoe! And how did I come here? And where had I been?' just as if he had been overjoyed to see me again; and so I carried him home along with me.

I had now had enough of rambling to sea for some time, and had enough to do for many days to sit still, and reflect upon the danger I had been in. I would have been very glad to have had my boat again on my side of the island; but I knew not how it was practicable to get it about. As to the east side of the island, which I had gone round, I knew well enough there was no venturing that way; my very heart would shrink, and my very blood run chill, but to think of it: and as to the other side of the island, I did not know how it might be there; but supposing the current ran with the same force against the shore at the east as it passed by it on the other, I might run the same risk of being driven down the stream, and carried by the island, as I had been before of being carried away from it; so with these thoughts I contented myself to be without any boat, though it had been the product of so many months' labour to make it, and of so many more to get it unto the sea.

In this government of my temper I remained near a year, lived a very sedate, retired life, as you may well suppose; and my thoughts being very much composed as to my condition, and fully comforted in resigning myself to the dispositions of Providence, I thought I lived really very happily in all things, except that of society.

I improved myself in this time in all the mechanic exercises which my necessities made me apply myself to, and I believe could, upon occasion, make a very good carpenter, especially considering how few tools I had.

I began now to perceive my powder abated considerably, and this was a want which it was impossible for me to supply, and I began seriously to consider what I must do when I should have no more powder; that is to say, how I should do to kill any goat. I had, as is observed in the third year of my being here, kept a young kid, and bred her up tame, and I was in hope of getting a he-goat, but I could not by any means bring it to pass, till my kid grew an old goat; and I could never find it in my heart to kill her, till she died at last of sheer age.

But being now in the eleventh year of my residence and, as I have said, my ammunition growing low, I set myself to study some art to trap and snare the goats, to see whether I could not catch some of them alive, and particularly I wanted a she-goat great with young.

To this purpose I made snares to hamper them, and I do believe they were more than once taken in them, but my tackle was not good, for I had no wire, and I always found them broken, and my bait devoured.

At length I resolved to try a pitfall; so I dug several large pits in the earth, in places where I had observed the goats used to feed, and over these pits I placed hurdles, of my own making too, with a great weight upon them; and several times I put ears of barley, and dry rice, without setting the trap, and I could easily perceive that the goats had gone in and eaten up the corn, for I could see the mark of their feet. At length I set three traps in one night, and going the next morning I found them all standing, and yet the bait eaten and gone; this was very discouraging. However, I altered my trap, and, not to trouble you with particulars, going one morning to see my trap, I found in one of them a large old he-goat, and in one of the other three kids, a male and two females.

As to the old one, I knew not what to do with him, he was so fierce I dared not go into the pit to him; that is to say, to go about to bring him away alive, which was what I wanted. I could have killed him, but that was not my business, nor would it answer my end. So I let him out, and he ran away as if he had been frightened out of his wits: but I had forgotten then what I learned afterwards, that hunger will tame a lion. If I had let him stay there three or four days without food, and then have carried him some water to drink, and then a little corn, he would have been as tame as one of the kids, for they are mighty tractable creatures where they are well used.

However, for the present I let him go, knowing no better at that time; then I went to the three kids, and taking them one by one, I tied them with strings together, and with some difficulty brought them all home.

It was a good while before they would feed, but throwing them some sweet corn, it tempted them and they began to be tame; and now I found that if I expected to supply myself with goat-flesh when I had no powder or shot left, breeding some up tame was my only way, when perhaps I might have them about my house like a flock of sheep.

In about a year and a half I had a flock of about twelve goats, kids and all; and in two years more I had three and forty, besides several that I took and killed for my food. And after that I enclosed five separate pieces of ground to feed them in, with little pens to drive them into, to take them as I wanted, and gates out of one piece of ground into another.

But this was not all, for now I not only had goat's flesh to feed on when I pleased, but milk too, a thing which indeed in my beginning I did not so much as think of, and which, when it came into my thoughts, was really an agreeable surprise. For now I set up my dairy, and had sometimes a gallon or two of milk in a day. And as nature, who gives supplies of food to every creature, dictates even naturally how to make use of it; so I that had never milked a cow, much less a goat, or seen butter or cheese made, very readily and handily, though after a great many essays and miscarriages, made me both butter and cheese at last, and never wanted it afterwards.

I was rather impatient, as I have observed, to have the use of my boat; though very loath to run any more hazards; and therefore sometimes I sat contriving ways to get her about the island, and at other times I sat myself down contented enough without her. But I had a strange uneasiness in my mind to go down to the point of the island, where, as I have said, in my last ramble, I went up the hill to see how the shore lay, and how the current set, than I might see what I had to do. This inclination increased upon me every day, and at length I resolved to travel thither by land, following the edge of the shore. I did so: but had anyone in England been to meet such a man as I was, it must either have frightened them, or raised a great deal of laughter; for, apart from my crudely made goat-skin clothes, on my travels I always carried pouches hung on a belt round my shoulder; at my back I carried my basket, on my shoulder my gun, and over my head a great, clumsy, ugly goat-skin umbrella, but which, after all, was the most necessary thing I had about me, next to my gun. My beard I had once allowed to grow till it was about a quarter of a yard long; but as I had both scissors and razors sufficient, I had cut it pretty short, except what grew on my upper lip, which I had trimmed into a large pair of whiskers; of these mustachioes or whiskers I will not say they were long enough to hang my hat upon them; but they were of a length and shape monstrous enough, and such as in England would have passed for frightful.

But all this is by the by; for as to my figure, I had so few to observe me that it was of no manner of consequence; so I say no more to that part. In this kind of figure I went my new journey, and was out five or six days. I travelled first along the sea-shore, directly to the place where I first brought my boat to anchor, to get up upon the rocks; and having no boat now to take care of, I went over the land a nearer way to the same height that I was upon before, when looking forward to the point of the rocks which lay out, and which I was obliged to double with my boat, as is said above, I was surprised to see the sea all smooth and quiet, no rippling, no motion, no current, any more there than in other places.

I was at a strange loss to understand this, and resolved to spend some time in observing it, to see if nothing from the sets of the tide had occasioned it; but I was presently convinced that the tide of ebb setting from the west, and joining with the current of waters from some great river on the shore, must be the occasion of this current; and that according as the wind blew more forcibly from the west or from the north, this current came nearer or went farther from the shore; for waiting thereabouts till evening, I went up to the rock again, and then the tide of ebb being made, I plainly saw the current again as before, only that it ran farther off, being near half a league from the shore; whereas in my case, it set close upon the shore, and hurried me and my canoe along with it, which at another time it would not have done.

This observation convinced me that I had nothing to do but to observe the ebbing and the flowing of the tide, and I might very easily bring my boat about the island again: but when I began to think of putting it in practice, I had such a terror upon my spirit at the remembrance of the danger I had been in, that I could not think of it again with any patience; but on the contrary, I took up another resolution which was more safe, though more laborious; and this was that I would build, or rather make me, another canoe; and so have one for one side of the island and one for the other.

You are to understand that now I had, as I may call it, two plantations in the island; one my little fortification or tent, with the wall about it under the rock, with the cave behind me, which by this time I had enlarged into several apartments or caves, one within another. One of these, which was dryest and largest, and had a door out beyond my wall or fortification, that is to say, beyond where my wall joined to the rock, was all filled up with large earthen pots, and with fourteen or fifteen great baskets, which would hold five or six bushels each, where I laid up my stores, especially my corn, some in the ear cut off short from the straw, and the other rubbed out with my hand.

As for my wall, made, as before, with long stakes or piles, those piles grew all like trees, and were by this time grown so big, and spread so very much, that there was not the least appearance to anyone's view of any habitation behind them.

Near this dwelling of mine, but a little farther within the land, and upon lower ground, lay my two pieces of corn-ground, which I kept duly cultivated and sown, and which duly yielded me their harvest in its season; and whenever I had occasion for more corn, I had more land adjoining as fit as that.

Besides this, I had my country seat, and I had now a tolerable plantation there also; for first, I had my little bower, as I called it, which I kept in repair; that is to say, I kept the hedge which circled it in constantly fitted up to its usual height, the ladder standing always in the inside; I kept the trees, which at first were no more than my stakes, but were now grown very firm and tall; I kept them always so cut, that they might spread and grow thick and wild, and make the more agreeable shade, which they did effectually to my mind. In the middle of this I had my tent always standing, being a piece of a sail spread over poles set up for that purpose, and which never wanted any repair or renewing; and under this I had made me a couch, with the skins of the creatures I had killed, and with other soft things, and a blanket laid on them, such as belonged to our sea-bedding, which I had saved, and a great watch-coat to cover me; and here, whenever I had occasion to be absent from my chief seat, I took up my country habitation.

Adjoining to this I had my enclosures for my goats. And as I had taken an inconceivable deal of pains to fence and enclose this ground, so I was so concerned to see it kept entire, lest the goats should break through, that I never left off till with infinite labour I had stuck the outside of the hedge so full of small stakes, and so near to one another, that it was rather a pale than a hedge, and there was scarce room to put a hand between them, which afterwards when those stakes grew, as they all did in the next rainy season, made the enclosure strong like a wall, indeed stronger than any wall.

This will testify that I was not idle, and that I spared no pains to bring to pass whatever appeared necessary for my comfortable support; for I considered the keeping up a breed of tame creatures thus at my hand would be a living source of flesh, milk, butter, and cheese for me as long as I lived in the place, if it were to be forty years; and that keeping them in my reach depended entirely upon my perfecting my enclosures to such a degree that I might be sure of keeping them together.

In this place also I had my grapes growing, which I principally depended on for my winter store of raisins, and which I never failed to preserve very carefully, as the best and most agreeable dainty of my whole diet; and indeed they were not agreeable only, but medicinal, wholesome, nourishing, and refreshing to the last degree.

As this was also about half-way between my other habitation and the place where I had laid up my boat, I generally stayed and lay here on my way thither; for I used frequently to visit my boat, and I kept all things about or belonging to her in very good order; sometimes I went out in her to divert myself, but no more hazardous voyages would I go, nor scarce ever above a stone's cast or two from the shore, I was so apprehensive of being hurried out of my knowledge again by the currents, or winds, or any other accident. But now I come to a new scene of my life.

## 8

It happened one day about noon going towards my boat, I was exceedingly surprised with the print of a man's naked foot on the shore, which was very plain to be seen in the sand. I stood like one thunder-struck, or as if I had seen a ghost; I listened, I looked round me, I could hear nothing, nor see anything; I went up to a rising ground to look farther; I went up the shore and down the shore, but it was all one, I could see no other impression but that one. I went to it again to see if there were any more, and to observe if it might not be my fancy; but there was no room for that, for there was exactly the very print of a foot, toes, heel, and every part of a foot; how it came thither I knew not, nor could in the least imagine. But after innumerable fluttering thoughts, like a man perfectly confused and out of myself, I came home to my fortification, not feeling, as we say, the ground I went on, but terrified to the last degree, looking behind me at every two or three steps, mistaking every bush and tree, and fancying every stump at a distance to be a man; nor is it possible to describe how many various shapes affrighted imagination represented things to me in, how many wild ideas were found every moment in my fancy, and what strange unaccountable whimsies came into my thoughts.

When I came to my castle, for so I think 1 called it ever after this, I fled into it like one pursued; whether I went over by the ladder as first contrived, or went in at the hole in the rock which I called a door, I cannot remember; no, nor could I remember the next morning, for never frightened hare fled to cover, or fox to earth, with more terror of mind than I to this retreat.

I slept none that night; the farther I was from the occasion of my fright, the greater my apprehensions were, which is somewhat contrary to the nature of such things, and especially to the usual practice of all creatures in fear: but I was so taken up with my own frightful ideas of the thing, that I formed nothing but dismal imaginations to myself, even though I was now a great way off of it. Sometimes I fancied it must be the devil; and reason joined in with me upon this supposition; for how should any other thing in human shape come into the place? Where was the vessel that brought them? What mark was there of any other footsteps? And how was it possible a man should come there? But then to think that Satan should take human shape upon him in such a place where there could be no manner of occasion for it, but to leave the print of his foot behind him, and that even for no purpose too, for he could not be sure

I should see it, this was a consideration the other way; I considered that the devil might have found out abundance of other ways to have terrified me than this of the single print of a foot; that as I lived quite on the other side of the island, he would never have been so simple to leave a mark in a place where 'twas ten thousand to one whether I should ever see it or not, and in the sand too, which the first surge of the sea upon a high wind would have defaced entirely. All this seemed inconsistent with the thing itself, and with all the notions we usually entertain of the subtlety of the devil.

Abundance of such things as these assisted to argue me out of all apprehensions of its being the devil; and I presently concluded then, that it must be some more dangerous creature – that it must be some of the savages of the mainland over against me, who had wandered out to sea in their canoes, and, either driven by the currents or by contrary winds, had made the island; and had been on shore, but were gone away again to sea, being as loath, perhaps, to have stayed in this desolate island as I would have been to have had them.

While these reflections were rolling upon my mind, I was very thankful in my thoughts that I was so lucky as not to be thereabouts at that time, or that they did not see my boat, by which they would have concluded that some inhabitants had been in the place, and perhaps have searched farther for me. Then terrible thoughts racked my imagination about their having found my boat, and that there were people here; and that if so, I should certainly have them come again in great numbers, and devour me; that if it should happen so that they should not find me, yet they would find my enclosure, destroy all my corn, carry away all my flock of tame goats, and I should perish at last for sheer want.

In the middle of these cogitations, apprehensions, and reflections, it came into my thought one day, that all this might be a mere chimera of my own, and that this foot might be the print of my own foot, when I came on shore from my boat. This cheered me up a little too, and I began to persuade myself it was all a delusion; that it was nothing else but my own foot, and why might not I come that way from the boat, as well as I was going that way to the boat? Again I considered also that I could by no means tell for certain where I had trod, and where I had not; and that if at last this was only the print of my own foot, I had played the part of those fools who strive to make stories of spectres and apparitions, and then are frightened at them more than anybody.

Now I began to take courage, and to peep abroad again; for I had not stirred out of my castle for three days and nights; so that I began to starve for provision; for I had little or nothing within doors but some barley cakes and water. Then I knew that my goats wanted to be milked too, which usually was my evening diversion; and the poor creatures were in great pain and inconvenience for want of it; and indeed, it almost spoiled some of them, and almost dried up their milk.

Heartening myself therefore with the belief that this was nothing but the print of one of my own feet, and so I might be truly said to start at my own shadow, I began to go abroad again, and went to my country house to milk my flock; but to see with what fear I went forward, how often I looked behind me, how I was ready every now and then to lay down my basket and run for my life, it would have made anyone have thought I was haunted with an evil conscience, or that I had been lately most terribly frightened, and so indeed I had.

However, as I went down thus two or three days, and having seen nothing, I began to be a little bolder, and to think there was really nothing in it but my own imagination: but I could not persuade myself fully of this till I should go down to the shore again, and see this print of a foot, and measure it by my own, and see if there was any similitude or fitness, that I might be assured it was my own foot. But when I came to the place, first, it appeared evident to me, that when I laid up my boat, I could not possibly be on shore anywhere thereabout; secondly, when I came to measure the mark with my own foot, I found my foot not so large by a great deal. Both these things filled my head with new imaginations, and gave me the vapours again to the highest degree; so that I shook with cold, like one in an ague; and I went home again, filled with the belief that some man or men had been on shore there; or in short, that the island was inhabited, and I might be surprised before I was aware; and what course to take for my security I knew not.

O what ridiculous resolution men take, when possessed with fear! It deprives them of the use of those means which reason offers for their relief. The first thing I proposed to myself was, to throw down my enclosures and turn all my tame cattle wild into the woods, that the enemy might not find them, and then frequent the island in prospect of the same, or the like booty; then to the simple thing of digging up my two corn-fields, that they might not find such a grain there, and still be prompted to frequent the island; then to demolish my bower and tent, that they might not see any vestiges of habitation, and be prompted to look farther, in order to find out the persons inhabiting.

These were the subject of the first night's cogitation, after I was come home again, while the apprehensions which had so overrun my mind were fresh upon me, and my head was full of vapours, as above. Thus fear of danger is ten thousand times more terrifying than danger itself when apparent to the eyes; and we find the burden of anxiety greater by much than the evil which we are anxious about.

This confusion of my thoughts kept me waking all night; but in the morning I fell asleep, and having, by the occupation of my mind, been as it were tired, and my spirits exhausted, I slept very soundly, and waked much better composed than I had ever been before; and now I began to think sedately; and upon the utmost debate with myself, I concluded that this island, which was so exceeding pleasant, fruitful, and no farther from the mainland than as I had seen, was not so entirely abandoned as I might imagine; that although there were no stated inhabitants who lived on the spot, yet that there might sometimes come boats off from the shore, who either with design, or perhaps never but when they were driven by cross winds, might come to this place.

That I had lived here fifteen years now, and had not met with the least shadow or figure of any people yet; and that if at any time they should be driven here, it was probable they went away again as soon as ever they could, seeing they had never thought fit to fix there upon any occasion, to this time.

That the most I could suggest any danger from, was from any such casual accidental landing of straggling people from the main, who, as it was likely if they were driven hither, were here against their wills, so they made no stay here, but went off again with all possible speed, seldom staying one night on shore, lest they should not have the help of the tides and daylight back again; and that therefore I had nothing to do but to consider of some safe retreat, in case I should see any savages land upon the spot.

Now I began sorely to repent that I had dug my cave so large as to bring a door through again, which door, as I said, came out beyond where my fortification joined to the rock; upon maturely considering this therefore, I resolved to draw me a second fortification, in the same manner of a semicircle, at a distance from my wall just where I had planted a double row of trees about twelve years before, of which I made mention. These trees having been planted so thick before, they wanted but a few piles to be driven between them, that they should be thicker and stronger, and my wall would be soon finished.

So that I had now a double wall, and my outer wall was thickened with pieces of timber, old cables, and everything I could think of, to make it strong; having in it seven little holes, about as big as I might put my arm out at. In the inside of this I thickened my wall to above ten foot thick, with continual bringing earth out of my cave, and laying it at the foot of the wall, and walking upon it; and through the seven holes I contrived to plant the muskets, of which I got seven on shore out of the ship; these, I say, I planted like my cannon, and fitted them into frames that held them like a carriage, that I could fire all the seven guns in two minutes' time. This wall I was many a weary month finishing, and yet never thought myself safe till it was done.

When this was done, I stuck all the ground without my wall, for a great way every way, as full with stakes or sticks of the osier-like wood, which I found so apt to grow, as they could well stand; insomuch that I believe I might set in near twenty thousand of them, leaving a pretty large space between them and my wall, that I might have room to see an enemy, and they might have no shelter from the young trees, if they attempted to approach my outer wall.

Thus in two years' time I had a thick grove, and in five or six years' time I had a wood before my dwelling, growing so monstrous thick and strong, that it was indeed perfectly impassable; and no men of what kind soever would ever imagine that there was anything beyond it, much less a habitation. As for the way which I proposed to myself to go in and out, for I left no avenue, it was setting two ladders, one to a part of the rock, which was low, and then broke in, and left room to place another ladder upon that; so when the two ladders were taken down, no man living could come down to me without injuring himself; and if they had come down they were still on the outside of my outer wall.

Thus I took all the measures human prudence could suggest for my own preservation; and it will be seen at length that they were not altogether without just reason; though I foresaw nothing at that time, more than my fear suggested to me.

While this was doing, I was not altogether careless of my other affairs; for I had a great concern upon me for my little herd of goats; they were not only a present supply to me upon every occasion, and began to be sufficient to me without the expense of powder and shot, but also without the fatigue of hunting after the wild ones, and I was loath to lose the advantage of them, and to have them all to nurse up over again.

To this purpose, after long consideration, I could think of but two ways to preserve them; one was to find another convenient place to dig a cave underground, and to drive them into it every night; and the other was to enclose two or three little bits of land remote from one another and as much concealed as I could, where I might keep about half a dozen young goats in each place: so that if any disaster happened to the flock in general, I might be able to raise them again with little trouble and time: and this, though it would require a great deal of time and labour, I thought was the most rational design.

Accordingly I spent some time to find out the most retired parts of the island; and I pitched upon one which was as private indeed as my heart could wish for; it was a little damp piece of ground in the middle of the hollow and thick woods, where, as is observed, I almost lost myself once before, endeavouring to come back that way from the eastern part of the island. Here I found a clear piece of land near three acres, so surrounded with woods that it was almost an enclosure by nature, at least it did not want near so much labour to make it so as the other pieces of ground I had worked so hard at.

I immediately went to work with this piece of ground, and in less than a month's time I had so fenced it round, that my flock or herd, call it which you please, who were not so wild now as at first they might have supposed to be, were well enough secured in it. So, without any farther delay, I removed ten young she-goats and two he-goats to this piece; and when they were there, I continued to perfect the fence till I had made it as secure as the other, which, however, I did at more leisure, and it took me up more time by a great deal.

All this labour I was at the expense of, purely from my apprehensions on the account of the print of a man's foot which I had seen; for as yet I never saw any human creature come near the island, and I had now lived two years under these uneasinesses.

After I had thus secured one part of my little living stock, I went about the whole island, searching for another private place, to make such another deposit; when wandering more to the west point of the island than I had ever gone yet, and looking out to sea, I thought I saw a boat upon the sea, at a great distance; I had found a perspective-glass or two in one of the seamen's chests, which I saved out of our ship; but I had it not about me, and this was so remote that I could not tell what to make of it, though I looked at it till my eyes were not able to look any longer; whether it was a boat or not, I do not know; but as I descended from the hill, I could see no more of it, so I gave it over; only I resolved to go no more out without a perspective-glass in my pocket.

When I was come down the hill to the end of the island, where indeed I had never been before, I was immediately convinced that seeing the print of a man's foot was not such a strange thing in the island as I imagined; and but that it was a special providence that I was cast upon the side of the island where the savages never came, I should easily have known that nothing was more frequent than for the canoes from the main, when they happened to be a little too far out at sea, to shoot over to that side of the island for harbour; likewise as they often met and fought in their canoes, the victors, having taken any prisoners, would bring them over to this shore, where according to their dreadful customs, being all cannibals, they would kill and eat them.

When I was come down the hill to the shore, as I said above, being the south-west point of the island, I was perfectly confounded and amazed; nor is it possible for me to express the horror of my mind, at seeing the shore spread with skulls, hands, feet, and other bones of human bodies; and particularly I observed a place where there had been a fire made, and a circle dug in the earth, where it is supposed the savage wretches had sat down to their inhuman feastings upon the bodies of their fellow-creatures.

I was so astonished with the sight of these things, that I entertained no notions of any danger to myself from it for a long while; all my apprehensions were buried in the thoughts of such a pitch of inhuman, hellish brutality, and the horror of the degeneracy of human nature; which, though I had heard of often, yet I never had so near a view of before; in short, I turned away my face from the horrid spectacle; my stomach grew sick, and I was just at the point of fainting, when nature discharged the disorder from my stomach, and having vomited with an uncommon violence, I was a little relieved, but could not bear to stay in the place a moment; so I went up the hill again with all the speed I could, and walked on towards my own habitation.

When I came a little out of that part of the island, I stood still awhile as amazed; and then recovering myself, I looked up with the utmost affection of my soul, and with a flood of tears in my eyes, gave God thanks that had cast my first lot in a part of the world where I was distinguished from such dreadful creatures as these; and that, though I had esteemed my present condition very miserable, had yet given me so many comforts in it, that I had still more to give thanks for than to complain of.

In this frame of thankfulness, I went home to my castle, and began to be much easier now, as to the safety of my circumstances, than ever I was before; for I observed that these wretches never came to this island in search of what they could get; perhaps not seeking, not wanting, or not expecting anything here; and having often, no doubt, been up in the covered woody part of it, without finding anything to their purpose. I knew I had been here now almost eighteen years, and never saw the least footsteps of human creature there before; and I might be here eighteen more, as entirely concealed as I was now, if I did not discover myself to them, which I had no manner of occasion to do, it being my only business to keep myself entirely concealed where I was, unless I found a better sort of creatures than cannibals to make myself known to.

Yet I entertained such an abhorrence of the savage wretches that I have been speaking of, and of the wretched inhuman custom of their devouring and eating one another up, that I continued pensive and sad, and kept close within my own circle for almost two years after this. When I say my own circle, I mean by it my three plantations – my castle, my country seat, which I called my bower, and my enclosure in the woods; nor did I look after this for any other purpose than as an enclosure for my goats; for the aversion which nature gave me to these hellish wretches was such, that I was as fearful of seeing them as of seeing the devil himself; nor did I so much as go to look after my boat in all this time, but began rather to think of making me another; for I could not think of ever making any more attempts to bring the other boat round the island to me, lest I should meet with some of the creatures at sea, in which if I happened to have fallen into their hands, I knew what would have been my lot.

Time, however, and the satisfaction I had that I was in no danger of being discovered by these people, began to wear off my uneasiness about them; and I began to live just in the same composed manner as before; only with this difference, that I used more caution, and kept my eyes more about me than I did before, lest I should happen to be seen by any of them; and particularly, I was more cautious of firing my gun, lest any of them being on the island should happen to hear it: and it was therefore a very good providence to me, that I had furnished myself with tame goats, that I needed not hunt any more about the woods, or shoot at them; and if I did catch any of them after this, it was by traps and snares, as I had done before; so that for two years after this, I believe I never fired my gun once off, though I never went out without it; and, which was more, as I had saved three pistols out of the ship, I always carried them out with me, or at least two of them, sticking them in my goat-skin belt; also I furbished up one of the great cutlasses that I had out of the ship, and made me a belt to put it on also; so that I was now a most formidable fellow to look at when I went abroad, if you add to the former description of myself, the particular of two pistols, and a great broadsword hanging at my side in a belt, but without a scabbard.

My invention now ran quite another way; for night and day I could think of nothing but how I might destroy some of these monsters in their cruel bloody entertainment, and, if possible, save the victim they should bring hither to destroy. It would take up a larger volume than this whole work is intended to be, to set down all the plans I hatched, or rather brooded upon in my thought, for the destroying these creatures, or at least frightening them, so as to prevent their coming hither any more; but all was abortive, nothing could be possible to take effect, unless I was to be there to do it myself; and what could one man do among them, when perhaps there might be twenty or thirty of them together, with their darts, or their bows and arrows, with which they could shoot as true to a mark as I could with my gun?

Sometimes I planned to dig a hole under the place where they made their fire, and put in five or six pound of gunpowder, which when they kindled their fire, would consequently take fire, and blow up all that was near it; but as in the first place I should be very loath to waste so much powder upon them, my store being now within the quantity of one barrel, so neither could I be sure of its going off at any certain time, when it might surprise them; and at best, that it would do little more than just blow the fire about their ears and frighten them; but not sufficient to make them forsake the place; so I laid it aside, and then proposed that I would place myself in ambush in some convenient place, with my three guns, all double loaded, and, in the middle of their bloody ceremony, let fly at them, when I should be sure to kill or wound perhaps two or three at every shot; and then falling in upon them with my three pistols and my sword, I made no doubt but that if there was twenty I should kill them all. This fancy pleased my thoughts for some weeks, and I was so full of it that I often dreamed of it, and sometimes that I was just going to let fly at them in my sleep.

I went so far with it in my imagination, that I employed myself several days to find out proper places to put myself in ambush, as I said, to watch for them; and I went frequently to the place itself, which was now grown more familiar to me; and especially while my mind was thus filled with thoughts of revenge, and of a bloody putting twenty or thirty of them to the sword, as I may call it, the horror I had at the place, and at the signs of the barbarous wretches devouring one another, abated my malice.

Well, at length I found a place in the side of the hill, where I was satisfied I might securely wait till I saw any of their boats coming, and might then, even before they would be ready to come on shore, convey myself unseen into thickets of trees, in one of which there was a hollow large enough to conceal me entirely; and where I might sit and observe all their bloody doings, and take my full aim at their heads, when they were so close together as that it would be next to impossible that I should miss, or that I could fail to wound three or four of them at the first shot.

In this place then I resolved to fix my design, and accordingly I prepared two muskets and my ordinary fowling-piece. The two muskets I loaded with a brace of slugs each, and four or five smaller bullets, about the size of pistol bullets; and the fowling-piece I loaded with near a handful of swan-shot, of the largest size; I also loaded my pistols with about four bullets each; and in this posture, well provided with ammunition for a second and third charge, I prepared myself for my expedition.

After I had thus laid the scheme of my design, and in my imagination put it in practice, I continually made my tour every morning up to the top of the hill, which was from my castle, as I called it, about three miles or more, to see if I could observe any boats upon the sea, coming near the island, or standing over towards it; but I began to tire of this hard duty, after I had for two or three months constantly kept my watch, but came always back without any discovery, there having not in all that time been the least appearance, not only on or near the shore, but not on the whole ocean, so far as my eyes or glasses could reach every way.

As long as I kept up my daily tour to the hill to look out, so long also I kept up the vigour of my design, and my spirits seemed to be all the while in a suitable form for so outrageous an execution as the killing twenty or thirty naked savages, for an offence which I had not at all entered into a discussion of in my thoughts, any farther than my passions were at first fired by the horror I conceived at the unnatural custom of that people. But now, when, as I have said, I began to be weary of the fruitless excursion, which I had made so long, and so far, every morning in vain, so my opinion of the action itself began to alter, and I began with cooler and calmer thoughts to consider what it was I was going to engage in; what authority or call I had, to pretend to be judge and executioner upon these men as criminals, whom Heaven had thought fit for so many ages to suffer unpunished. I debated this very often with myself thus: How do I know what God Himself judges in this particular case? It is certain these people do not commit this as a crime; thcy do not know it be an offence, and then commit in defiance of divine justice, as we do in almost all the sins we commit. They think it no more a crime to kill a captive taken in war, than we do to kill an ox; nor to eat human flesh, than we do to eat mutton.

In the next place it occurred to me, that albeit

the usage they thus gave one another was brutish and inhuman, yet it was really nothing to me: these people had done me no injury. That if they attempted me, or I saw it necessary for my immediate preservation to fall upon them, something might be said for it; but that I was yet out of their power, and they had really no knowledge of me, and consequently no design upon me; and therefore it could not be just for me to fall upon them.

These considerations really put me to a pause, and to a kind of a full stop; and I began by little and little to be off of my design, and to conclude I had taken wrong measures in my resolutions to attack the savages; that it was not my business to meddle with them, unless they first attacked me, and this it was my business if possible to prevent; but that if I were discovered and attacked, then I knew my duty.

On the other hand, I argued with myself, that this really was the way not to deliver myself, but entirely to ruin and destroy myself; for unless I was sure to kill every one that not only should be on shore at that time, but that should ever come on shore afterwards, if but one of them escaped to tell their people what had happened, they would come over again by thousands to revenge the death of their fellows, and I should only bring upon myself a certain destruction.

Upon the whole I concluded that neither in principle or in policy, I ought one way or other to concern myself in this affair. That my business was by all possible means to conceal myself from them, and not to leave the least sign to them to guess by, that there were any living creatures upon the island; I mean of human shape.

## 9

In this disposition I continued for near a year
after this; and so far was I from desiring an
occasion for falling upon these wretches, that in
all that time I never once went up the hill to see
whether there were any of them in sight, or to
know whether any of them had been on shore
there or not, that I might not be tempted to renew
any of my contrivances against them, or be pro-
voked by any advantage which might present
itself, to fall upon them; only this I did, I went
and removed my boat, which I had on the other
side of the island, and carried it down to the east
end of the whole island, where I ran it into a little
cove which I found under some high rocks, and
where I knew, by reason of the currents, the
savages would not come with their boats, upon
any account whatsoever.

Besides this, I kept myself, as I said, more
retired than ever, and seldom went from my cell,
other than upon my constant employment, to milk
my she-goats, and manage my little flock in the
wood; which, as it was quite on the other part of
the island, was quite out of danger; for certain it

is, that these savage people who sometimes haunted this island never came with any thoughts of finding anything here; and consequently never wandered off from the coast; and I doubt not, but they might have been several times on shore after my apprehensions of them had made me cautious, as well as before; and indeed, I looked back with some horror upon the thoughts of what my condition would have been, if I had chanced upon them and been discovered before that, when naked and unarmed, except with one gun, and that loaded often only with small-shot, I walked everywhere peeping and peeping about the island to see what I could get; what a surprise should I have been in, if when I discovered the print of a man's foot, I had instead of that seen fifteen or twenty savages, and found them pursuing me, and by the swiftness of their running, no possibility of my escaping them.

The thoughts of this sometimes sunk my very soul within me, and distressed my mind so much, that I could not soon recover it, to think what I should have done, and how I not only should not have been able to resist them, but even should not have had presence of mind enough to do what I might have done; much less, what now after so much consideration and preparation I might be able to do. Indeed, after serious thinking of these things, I could be very melancholy; and sometimes it would last a great while; but I resolved it at last all into thankfulness to that Providence, which had delivered me from so many unseen dangers, and had kept me from those mischiefs which I could no way have been the agent in delivering myself from.

I believe the reader of this will not think it strange if I confess that these anxieties, these constant dangers I lived in, and the concern that was now upon me, put an end to all invention, and to all the contrivances that I had laid for my future accommodations and conveniences. I had the care of my safety more now upon my hands than that of my food. I cared not to drive a nail or chop a stick of wood now, for fear the noise I should make should be heard; much less would I fire a gun, for the same reason; and above all, I was intolerably uneasy at making any fire, lest the smoke which is visible at a great distance in the day should betray me; and for this reason I removed that part of my business which required fire, such as burning of pots and pipes, into my new apartment in the woods, where, after I had been some time, I found, to my unspeakable consolation, a completely natural cave in the earth, which went in a vast way, and where, I dare say, no savage, had he been at the mouth of it, would be so hardy as to venture in, nor indeed would any man else, but one who, like me, wanted nothing so much as a safe retreat.

The mouth of this hollow was at the bottom of a great rock, where by sheer accident (I would say, if I did not see abundant reason to ascribe all such things now to Providence) I was cutting down some thick branches of trees, to make charcoal; and before I go on, I must observe the reason of my making this charcoal; which was thus:

I was afraid of making a smoke about my habitation, as I said before; and yet I could not live there without baking my bread, cooking my meat, etc., so I contrived to burn some wood here, as I had seen done in England, under turf, till it became chark, or dry coal; and then putting the fire out, I preserved the coal to carry home, and perform the other services which fire was wanting for at home without danger of smoke.

But this is by the by. While I was cutting down some wood here, I perceived that behind a very thick branch of low brushwood, there was a kind of hollow place; I was curious to look into it, and getting with difficulty into the mouth of it, I found it was pretty large; that is to say, sufficient for me to stand upright in it, and perhaps another with me; but I must confess to you, I made more haste out than I did in, when looking farther into the place, which was perfectly dark, I saw two broad shining eyes of some creature, whether devil or man I knew not, which twinkled like two stars, the dim light from the cave's mouth shining directly in and making the reflection.

However, after some pause, I recovered myself, and began to call myself a thousand fools, and tell myself, that he that was afraid to see the devil was not fit to live twenty years in an island all alone; and that no doubt there was nothing in this cave that was more frightful than myself; upon this, plucking up my courage, I took up a great fire-brand, and in I rushed again, with the stick flaming in my hand. I had not gone three steps in, but I was almost as much frightened as I was before; for I heard a very loud sigh, like that of a man in some pain, and it was followed by a broken noise, as if words half expressed, and then a deep sigh again. I stepped back, and was indeed struck with such a surprise, that it put me into a cold sweat; and if I had had a hat on my head, I will not answer for it, that my hair might not have lifted it off. But still plucking up my spirits as well as I could, and encouraging myself a little with considering that the power and presence of God was everywhere, and was able to protect me; upon this I stepped forward again, and by the light of the firebrand, holding it up a little over my head, I saw lying on the ground a most monstrous frightful old he-goat, just making his will, as we say, and gasping for life, and dying in fact of old age.

I stirred him a little to see if I could get him out, and he tried to get up, but was not able to raise himself; and I thought with myself, he might even lie there; for if he had frightened me so, he would certainly frighten any of the savages, if any of them should be so hardy as to come in there, while he had any life in him.

I was now recovered from my surprise, and

began to look round me, when I found the cave was but very small, that is to say, it might be about twelve foot over, but in no manner of shape, either round or square, no hands having ever been employed in making it but those of nature. I observed also, that there was a place at the farther side of it, that went in farther, but was so low that it required me to creep upon my hands and knees to go into it, and whither I went I knew not; so having no candle, I gave it over for some time; but resolved to come again the next day, provided with candles and a tinderbox, which I had made of the lock of one of the muskets.

Accordingly, the next day I came provided with six large candles of my own making; for I made very good candles now of goat's tallow; and going into this low place, I was obliged to creep upon all fours, as I have said, almost ten yards; which, by the way, I thought was a venture bold enough, considering that I knew not how far it might go, nor what was beyond it. When I was got through the strait, I found the roof rose higher up, I believe near twenty foot; but never was such a glorious sight seen in the island, I dare say, as it was to look round the sides and roof of this vault or cave; the walls reflected a hundred thousand lights to me from my two candles; what it was in the rock, whether diamonds, or any other precious stones, or gold, which I rather supposed it to be, I knew not.

The place I was in was a most delightful cavity

or grotto of its kind, as could be expected, though perfectly dark; the floor was dry and level, and had a sort of small loose gravel upon it, so that there was no nauseous or venomous creature to be seen, neither was there any damp or wet on the sides or roof. The only difficulty in it was the entrance, which, however, as it was a place of security, and such a retreat as I wanted, I thought was a convenience; so that I was really delighted at the discovery, and resolved without any delay to bring some of those things which I was most anxious about, to this place; particularly, I resolved to bring hither my store of powder, and two fowling-pieces, for I had three in all; and three muskets, for of them I had eight in all; so I kept at my castle only five, which stood ready mounted like pieces of cannon on my outmost fence, and were ready also to take out upon any expedition.

Upon this occasion of removing my ammunition, I took occasion to open the barrel of powder which I took up out of the sea, and which had been wet and I found that the water had penetrated about three or four inches into the powder on every side, which caking and growing hard, had preserved the inside like a kernel in a shell; so that I had near sixty pound of very good powder in the centre of the cask, and this was an agreeable discovery to me at that time; so I carried all away thither, never keeping above two or three pound of powder with me in my castle, for fear of a surprise of any kind: I also carried thither all the lead I had left for bullets.

I fancied myself now like one of the ancient giants, which are said to live in caves and holes in the rocks, where none could come at them; for I persuaded myself while I was here, if five hundred savages were to hunt me, they could never find me out; or if they did, they would not venture to attack me here.

The old goat who I found expiring died in the mouth of the cave, the next day after I made this discovery; and I found it much easier to dig a great hole there, and throw him in and cover him with earth, than to drag him out; so I interred him there, to prevent the offence to my nose.

I was now in my twenty-third year of residence in this island, and was so naturalized to the place, and to the manner of living, that could I have but enjoyed the certainty that no savages would come to the place to disturb me, I could have been content to have capitulated for spending the rest of my time there, even to the last moment, till I had laid me down and died, like the old goat in the cave.

But it was otherwise directed. It was now the month of December, in my twenty-third year; and this being the southern solstice, for winter I cannot call it, was the particular time of my harvest, and required my being pretty much abroad in the fields; when going out pretty early in the morning, even before it was fully daylight, I was surprised with seeing a light of some fire upon the shore, at a distance from me of about two mile towards the end of the island, where I had observed some savages had been as before; but not on the other side; but to my great affliction, it was on my side of the island.

I was indeed terribly surprised at the sight, and stopped short within my grove, not daring to go out, lest I might be surprised; and yet I had no more peace within, from the apprehensions I had that if these savages, in rambling over the island, should find my corn standing or cut, or any of my works and improvements, they would immediately conclude that there were people in the place, and would then never give over till they had found me out. In this extremity I went back directly to my castle, pulled up the ladder after me, and made all things without look as wild and natural as I could.

Then I prepared myself within, putting myself in a posture of defence; I loaded all my cannon, as I called them, that is to say, my muskets which were mounted upon my new fortification, and all my pistols, and resolved to defend myself to the last gasp, not forgetting seriously to commend myself to the divine protection, and earnestly to pray to God to deliver me out of the hands of the barbarians; and in this posture I continued about two hours; but began to be mighty impatient for intelligence abroad, for I had no spies to send out.

After sitting a while longer, and musing what I should do in this case, I was not able to bear sitting in ignorance any longer; so setting up my ladder to the side of the hill, where there was a flat place, as I observed before, and then pulling the ladder up after me, I set it up again, and mounted to the top of the hill; and pulling out my perspective-glass, which I had taken on purpose, I laid me down flat on my belly on the ground, and began to look for the place; I presently found there were no less than nine naked savages, sitting round a small fire they had made, not to warm them, for they had no need of that, the weather being extreme hot; but, as I supposed, to dress some of their barbarous diet of human flesh, which they had brought with them, whether alive or dead I could not know.

They had two canoes with them, which they had hauled up upon the shore; and as it was then tide of ebb, they seemed to me to wait for the return of the flood, to go away again; it is not easy to imagine what confusion this sight put me into, especially seeing them come on my side the island, and so near me too; but when I observed their coming must always be with the current of the ebb, I began afterwards to be more sedate in my mind, being satisfied that I might go abroad with safety all the time of the tide of flood, if they were not on shore before: and having made this observation, I went abroad about my harvest work with the more composure.

As I expected, so it proved; for as soon as the

tide made to the westward, I saw them all take boat, and paddle away.

As soon as I saw them shipped and gone, I took two guns upon my shoulders, and two pistols at my girdle, and my great sword by my side, without a scabbard, and with all the speed I was able to make, I went away to the hill, where I had discovered the first appearance of all; and as soon as I got there, which was not less than two hours (for I could not go apace, being so laden with arms), I perceived there had been three canoes more of savages in that place; and looking out farther, I saw they were all at sea together, making over for the main.

This was a dreadful sight to me, especially when going down to the shore, I could see the marks of horror which the dismal work they had been about had left behind it – the blood, the bones, and part of the flesh of human bodies, eaten and devoured by those wretches, with merriment and sport. I was so filled with indignation at the sight, that I began now to premeditate the destruction of the next that I saw there, let them be who or how many soever.

It seemed evident to me that the visits which they thus make to this island are not very frequent; for it was above fifteen months before any more of them came on shore there again; but in the month of May, as near as I could calculate, and in my four and twentieth year, I had a very strange encounter with them, of which in its place.

The perturbation of my mind, during this fifteen or sixteen months' interval, was very great; I slept unquiet, dreamed always frightful dreams, and often started out of my sleep in the night: in the day great troubles overwhelmed my mind, and in the night I dreamed often of killing the savages, and of the reasons why I might justify the doing of it; but to wave all this for a while, it was in the middle of May, on the sixteenth day I think, as well as my poor wooden calendar would reckon; for I marked all upon the post still; I say, it was the sixteenth of May, that it blew a very great storm of wind all day, with a great deal of lightning and thunder, and a very foul night it was after it; I know not what was the particular occasion of it, but as I was reading in the Bible, and taken up with very serious thoughts about my present condition, I was surprised with a noise of a gun, as I thought, fired at sea.

This was to be sure a surprise of a quite different nature from any I had met with before; for the notions this put into my thoughts were quite of another kind. I started up in the greatest haste imaginable, and in a trice clapped my ladder to the middle place of the rock, and pulled it after me, and mounting it the second time, got to the top of the hill the very moment that a flash of fire bid me listen for a second gun, which accordingly in about half a minute I heard, and by the sound knew that it was from that part of the sea where I was driven down the current in my boat.

I immediately considered that this must be some ship in distress, and that they had some comrade, or some other ship in company, and fired these guns for signals of distress, and to obtain help. I had this presence of mind at that minute, as to think that though I could not help them, it may be they might help me; so I brought together all the dry wood I could get at hand, and making a good handsome pile, I set it on fire upon the hill; the wood was dry, and blazed freely; I was certain, if there was any such thing as a ship, they must needs see it, and no doubt they did; for as soon as ever my fire blazed up, I heard another gun, and after that several others, all from the same quarter; I plied my fire all night long, till day broke; and when it was broad day, and the air cleared up, I saw something at a great distance at sea, full east of the island, whether a sail or a hull I could not distinguish, no, not with my glasses, the distance was so great, and the weather still rather hazy also; at least it was so out at sea.

I looked frequently at it all that day, and soon perceived that it did not move; so I presently concluded that it was a ship at anchor, and being eager, you may be sure, to be satisfied, I took my gun in my hand, and ran toward the south side of the island, to the rocks where I had formerly been carried away with the current; and getting up there, the weather by this time being perfectly clear, I could plainly see, to my great sorrow, the wreck of a ship cast away in the night upon those concealed rocks which I found when I was out in my boat; and which rocks, as they checked the violence of the stream and made a kind of counter-stream or eddy, were the occasion of my recovering from the most desperate hopeless condition that ever I had been in in all my life.

Thus what is one man's safety is another man's destruction; for it seems these men, whoever they were, being out of their knowledge, and the rocks being wholly underwater, had been driven upon them in the night, the wind blowing hard at E and ENE. Had they seen the island, as I must necessarily suppose they did not, they must, as I thought, have endeavoured to have saved themselves on shore by the help of their boat; but their firing of guns for help, especially when they saw, as I imagined, my fire, filled me with many thoughts. First, I imagined that upon seeing my light, they might have put themselves into their boat, and have endeavoured to make the shore; but that the sea going very high, they might have been cast away; other times I imagined they might have lost their boat before, as might be the case many ways; as particularly by the breaking of the sea upon their ship, which many times obliges men to stave or take in pieces their boat, and sometimes to throw it overboard with their own hands; other times I imagined they had some other ship or ships in company, who, upon the signals of distress they had made, had taken them up and carried them off; other whiles I fancied they were all gone off to sea in their boat, and being hurried away by the current that I had been formerly in, were carried out into the great ocean, where there was nothing but misery and perishing; and that perhaps they might by this time think of starving, and of being in a condition to eat one another.

I cannot explain by any possible energy of words what a strange longing or hankering of desires I felt in my soul upon this sight; breaking out sometimes thus: 'O that there had been but one or two; nay, or but one soul saved out of this ship, to have escaped to me, that I might but have had one companion, one fellow-creature to have spoken to me, and to have conversed with!' In all the time of my solitary life, I never felt so earnest, so strong a desire after the society of my fellow-creatures, or so deep a regret at the want of it.

But it was not to be; either their fate or mine, or both, forbade it; for till the last year of my being on this island, I never knew whether any were saved out of that ship or no; and had only the affliction, some days after, to see the corpse of a drowned boy come on shore, at the end of the island which was next to the shipwreck. He had on no clothes but a seaman's waistcoat, a pair of open-kneed linen drawers, and a blue linen shirt; but nothing to direct me so much as to guess what nation he was of. He had nothing in his pocket but two pieces of eight, and a tobacco-pipe; that last was to me of ten times more value than the first.

It was now calm, and I had a great mind to venture out in my boat to this wreck; not doubting but I might find something on board that might be useful to me; but that did not altogether press me so much as the possibility that there might yet be some living creature on board, whose life I might not only save, but might, by saving that life, comfort my own to the last degree; and this thought clung so to my heart, that I could not be quiet, night or day, but I must venture out in my boat on board this wreck; and committing the rest to God's providence, I thought the impression was so strong upon my mind, that it could not be resisted, that it must come from some invisible direction, and that I should be untrue to myself if I did not go.

Under the power of this impression, I hastened back to my castle, prepared everything for my voyage, took a quantity of bread, a great pot for fresh water, a compass to steer by, a bottle of rum, for I had still a great deal of that left, a basket full of raisins; and thus loading myself with everything necessary, I went down to my boat, got the water out of her, and got her afloat, loaded all my cargo in her, and then went home again for more; my second cargo was a great bag full of rice, the umbrella to set up over my head for shade, another large pot full of fresh water, and about two dozen of my small loaves of barley cakes, more than before, with a bottle of goat's milk and a cheese; all which, with great labour and sweat, I brought to my boat; and praying to God to direct my voyage, I put out, and rowing the canoe along the shore, I came at last to the utmost point of the island on that north-east side. And now I was to launch out into the ocean, and either to venture, or not to venture. I looked on the rapid currents which ran constantly on both sides of the island at a distance, and which were very terrible to me, from the remembrance of the hazard I had been in before, and my heart began to fail me; for I foresaw that if I was driven into either of those currents, I should be carried a vast way out to sea, and perhaps out of my reach, or sight of the island again; and that then, as my boat was but small, if any little wind should rise, I should be inevitably lost.

These thoughts so oppressed my mind that I began to give over my enterprise, and having hauled my boat into a little creek on the shore, I stepped out and sat me down upon a little rising bit of ground, very pensive and anxious, between fear and desire about my voyage; when, as I was musing, I could perceive that the tide was turned, and the flood come on, upon which my going was for so many hours impracticable; upon this presently it occurred to me that I should go up to the highest piece of ground I could find, and observe, if I could, how the sets of the tide or currents lay when the flood came in, that I might judge whether, if I was driven one way out, I might not expect to be driven another way home, with the same rapidness of the currents. This thought was no sooner in my head, but I cast my eye upon a little hill, which sufficiently overlooked the sea both ways, and from whence I had a clear view of the currents, or sets of the tide, and which way I was to guide myself in my return; here I found, that as the current of the ebb set out close by the south point of the island, so the current of the flood set in close by the shore of the north side, and that I had nothing to do but to keep to the north of the island in my return, and I should do well enough.

Encouraged with this observation, I resolved the next morning to set out with the first of the tide; and having spent the night in the canoe, I launched out. I made first a little out to sea full north, till I began to feel the benefit of the current, which set eastward, and which carried me at a great rate, and yet did not so hurry me as the southern-side current had done before, and so as to take from me all government of the boat; but having a strong steerage with my paddle, I went at a great rate directly for the wreck, and in less than two hours I came up to it.

It was a dismal sight to look at: the ship, which by its building was Spanish, stuck fast, jammed in between two rocks; all the stern and quarter of her was beaten to pieces by the sea; and as her forecastle, which stuck in the rocks, had run on with great violence, her mainmast and foremast were broken short off; but her boltsprit was sound and the head and bow appeared firm.

I went on board: but the first sight I met with was two men drowned in the cook-room or forecastle of the ship, with their arms fast about one another. I concluded, as is indeed probable, that when the ship struck, it being in a storm, the sea broke so high and continually over her, that the men were not able to bear it, and were strangled with the constant rushing in of the water, as much as if they had been underwater. There was nothing left in the ship that had life; nor any goods that I could see, but what were spoiled by the water. There were some casks of liquor, whether wine or brandy I knew not, which lay lower in the hold, and which, the water being ebbed out, I could see; but they were too big to meddle with. I saw several chests, which I believed belonged to some of the seamen; and I got two of them into the boat, without examining what was in them.

I found, besides these chests, a little cask full of liquor, of about twenty gallons, which I got into my boat with much difficulty; there were several muskets in a cabin, and a great powder-horn, with about four pounds of powder in it; as for the muskets, I had no occasion for them; so I left them, but took the powder-horn. I took a fire shovel and tongs, which I wanted extremely; as also two little brass kettles, a copper pot to make chocolate, and a gridiron; and with this cargo I came away, the tide beginning to make home again; and the same evening, about an hour within night, reached the island again, weary and fatigued to the last degree.

I reposed that night in the boat, and in the morning I resolved to harbour what I had got in my new cave, not to carry it home to my castle. After refreshing myself, I got all my cargo on shore, and began to examine the particulars. The cask of liquor I found to be a kind of rum, but not at all good; but when I came to open the chest, I found several things of great use to me: for example, I found in one a fine case of bottles, of an extraordinary kind, and filled with cordial waters, fine and very good; the bottles held about three pints each, and were tipped with silver: I found two pots of very good sweetmeats, so fastened also on top that the salt water had not hurt them; and two more of the same, which the water had spoiled: I found some very good shirts, which were very welcome to me; and about a dozen and half of linen white handkerchiefs and coloured neck-cloths; the former were also very welcome, being exceeding refreshing to wipe my face in a hot day. Besides this, when I came to the till in the chest, I found there three great bags of pieces of eight, which held about eleven hundred pieces in all; and in one of them, wrapped up in a paper, six doubloons of gold, and some small bars or wedges of gold; I suppose they might all weigh near a pound.

Upon the whole, I got very little by this voyage

that was of any use to me; for as to the money, I had no manner of occasion for it: 'twas to me as the dirt under my feet; and I would have given it all for three or four pair of English shoes and stockings, which were things I greatly wanted, but had not had on my feet now for many years: I had indeed got two pair of shoes now, which I took off the feet of the two drowned men who I saw in the wreck; and I found two pair more in one of the chests, which were very welcome to me; but they were not like our English shoes, either for ease or service; being rather what we call pumps than shoes. I found in the other chest about fifty pieces of eight in ryals, but no gold; I suppose this belonged to a poorer man than the other, which seemed to belong to some officer.

Well, however, I lugged this money home to my cave, and laid it up as I had done that before which I brought from our own ship. Having now brought all my things on shore, and secured them, I went back to my boat, and paddled her along the shore to her old harbour, where I laid her up, and made the best of my way to my old habitation, where I found everything safe and quiet; so I began to repose myself, live after my old fashion, and take care of my family affairs; and for a while, I lived easy enough; only that I was more vigilant than I used to be, looked out oftener, and did not go abroad so much; and if at any time I did stir with any freedom, it was always to the east part of the island, where I was pretty well satisfied the savages never came, and where I could go without so many precautions, and such a load of arms and ammunition as I always carried with me if I went the other way.

I lived in this condition near two years more; but my unlucky head, that was always to let me know it was born to make my body miserable, was all this two years filled with projects and designs, how, if it were possible, I might get away from this island; for sometimes I was for making another voyage to the wreck, though my reason told me that there was nothing left there worth the hazard of my voyage; sometimes for a ramble one way, sometimes another; and I believe verily, if I had had the boat that I went from Sallee in, I should have ventured to sea, bound anywhere, I knew not whither.

I have been in all my circumstances a memento to those who are touched with the general plague of mankind; I mean that of not being satisfied with the station wherein God and nature has placed them; I was continually poring upon the means and possibility of my escape from this place.

One night I dreamed that as I was going out in the morning as usual from my castle, I saw upon the shore two canoes and eleven savages coming to land, and that they brought with them another savage, who they were going to kill, in order to eat him; when on a sudden, the savage that they were going to kill, jumped away, and ran for his life;

and I thought, in my sleep, that he came running into my little thick grove before my fortification, to hide himself; and that I seeing him alone, and not perceiving that the others sought him that way, showed myself to him, and smiling upon him, encouraged him; that he kneeled down to me, seeming to pray me to assist him; upon which I showed my ladder, made him go up and carried him into my cave, and he became my servant; and that as soon as I had got this man, I said to myself, 'Now I may certainly venture to the mainland; for this fellow will serve me as a pilot, and will tell me what to do, and whether not to go for fear of being devoured, what places to venture into, and what to escape.' I waked with this thought, and was under such inexpressible impression of joy at the prospect of my escape in my dream, that the disappointments which I felt upon coming to myself and finding it was no more than a dream, were equally extravagant the other way, and threw me into a very great dejection of spirit.

Upon this, however, I made this conclusion, that my only way to go about an attempt for an escape was, if possible, to get a savage into my possession; and if possible, it should be one of their prisoners, who they had condemned to be eaten, and should bring thither to kill; but these thoughts still were attended with this difficulty, that it was impossible to effect this, without attacking a whole caravan of them, and killing them all; and this was not only a very desperate attempt, and might miscarry; but on the other hand, I had greatly scrupled the lawfulness of it to me; and my heart trembled at the thoughts of shedding so much blood, though it was for my deliverance.

However, at last, after many secret disputes with myself, and after great perplexities about it, for all these arguments one way and another struggled in my head a long time, the eager prevailing desire of deliverance at length mastered all the rest; and I resolved, if possible, to get one of those savages into my hands, cost what it would. My next thing then was to contrive how to do it, and this indeed was very difficult to resolve on. But as I could pitch upon no probable means for it, so I resolved to put myself upon the watch, to see them when they came on shore, and leave the rest to the event, taking such measures as the opportunity should present, let be what would be.

With these resolutions in my thoughts, I set myself upon the scout as often as possible, and indeed so often till I was heartily tired of it, for it was above a year and a half that I waited, and for great part of that time went out to the west end, and to the south-west corner of the island, almost every day, to look for canoes, but none appeared. This was very discouraging, and began to trouble me much, though I cannot say that it did in this case, as it had done some time before that, wear off the edge of my desire to the thing. But the longer it seemed to be delayed, the more eager I was for it; in a word, I was not at first so careful to shun the sight of these savages, and avoid being seen by them, as I was now eager to be upon them.

## 10

About a year and a half after I had entertained these notions, I was surprised one morning early, with seeing no less than five canoes all on shore together on my side of the island; and the people who belonged to them all landed, and out of my sight. The number of them broke all my measures, for seeing so many, and knowing that they always came four or six, or sometimes more in a boat, I could not tell what to think of it, or how to attack twenty or thirty men single-handed; so I lay still in my castle, perplexed and discomforted; however, I put myself into all the same postures for an attack that I had formerly provided, and was just ready for action, if anything had presented. Having waited a good while, listening to hear if they made any noise, at length, being very impatient, I set my guns at the foot of my ladder, and clambered up to the top of the hill; standing so, however, that my head did not appear above the hill, so that they could not perceive me by any means; here I observed, by the help of my perspective-glass, that they were no less than thirty in number, that they had a fire kindled, that they had had meat dressed. How they cooked it, that I knew not, or what it was; but they were all dancing in I know not how many barbarous gestures and figures, their own way, round the fire.

While I was thus looking on them, I perceived two miserable wretches dragged from the boats, where it seems they were laid by, and were now brought out for the slaughter. I perceived one of them immediately fall, being knocked down, I suppose with a club or wooden sword, for that was their way, and two or three others were at work immediately cutting him open for their cookery, while the other victim was left standing by himself, till they should be ready for him. In that very moment this poor wretch seeing himself a little at liberty, nature inspired him with hopes of life, and he started away from them, and ran with incredible swiftness along the sands directly towards me, I mean towards that part of the coast where my habitation was.

I was dreadfully frightened (that I must acknowledge) when I perceived him to run my way, and especially when, as I thought, I saw him pursued by the whole body; and now I expected that part of my dream was coming to pass, and that he would certainly take shelter in my grove; but I could not depend by any means upon my dream for the rest of it – that the other savages would not pursue him thither, and find him there. However, I kept my station, and my spirits began to recover when I found that only three men followed him, and still more was I encouraged when I found that he outstripped them exceedingly in running, and gained ground of them, so that if he could but hold it for half an hour, I saw easily he would fairly get away from them all.

There was between them and my castle the creek which I mentioned at the first part of my story; and this, I saw plainly, he must necessarily swim over, or the poor wretch would be taken there. But when the savage escaping came thither, he made nothing of it, though the tide was then up, but plunging in, swam through in about thirty strokes or thereabouts, landed, and ran on with exceeding strength and swiftness; when the three persons came to the creek, I found that two of them could swim, but the third could not, and that standing on the other side, he looked at the other, but went no further, and soon after went softly back again, which, as it happened, was very well for him in the main.

I observed that the two who swam were yet more than twice as long swimming over the creek as the fellow was that fled from them. It came now very warmly upon my thought, and indeed irresistibly, that now was my time to get me a servant, and perhaps a companion or assistant; and that I was called plainly by Providence to save this poor creature's life; I immediately ran down the ladders with all possible expedition, fetched my two guns, for they were both but at the foot of the ladders, as I observed above; and

getting up again, with the same haste, to the top
of the hill, I crossed toward the sea; and having a
very short cut, and all downhill, thrust myself in
the way between the pursuers and the pursued;
shouting aloud to him that fled, who looking back,
was at first perhaps as much frightened at me
as at them; but I beckoned with my hand to him
to come back; and in the meantime, I slowly
advanced towards the two that followed; then
rushing at once upon the foremost, I knocked
him down with the stock of my piece; I was loath
to fire, because I would not have the rest hear;
though at that distance it would not have been
easily heard, and being out of sight of the smoke
too, they would not have easily known what to
make of it. Having knocked this fellow down, the
other who pursued with him stopped, as if he had
been frighted; and I advanced apace towards him;
but as I came nearer, I perceived he had a bow
and arrow, and was fitting it to shoot at me; so I
was then necessitated to shoot at him first, which
I did, and killed him at the first shot; the poor
savage who fled, but had stopped, though he saw
both his enemies fallen and killed, as he thought,
yet was so frightened with the fire and noise of
my piece, that he stood stock still, and neither
came forward or went backward, though he
seemed rather inclined to fly still than to come on;
I called again to him, and made signs to come
forward, which he easily understood, and came a
little way, then stopped again, and then a little

further, and stopped again, and I could then perceive that he stood trembling, as if he had been
taken prisoner, and had just been to be killed, as
his two enemies were. I beckoned him again to
come to me, and gave him all the signs of encouragement that I could think of, and he came nearer
and nearer, kneeling down every ten or twelve
steps in token of acknowledgement for my saving
his life. I smiled at him, and looked pleasantly,
and beckoned to him to come still nearer; at length
he came close to me, and then he kneeled down
again, kissed the ground, and laid his head upon
the ground, and taking me by the foot, set my foot
upon his head; this it seems was in token of
swearing to be my slave for ever; I took him up,
and made much of him, and encouraged him all I
could. But there was more work to do yet, for I
perceived the savage who I knocked down was not
killed, but stunned with the blow, and began to
come to himself; so I pointed to him, and showing
him the savage, that he was not dead; upon this he
spoke some words to me, and though I could not
understand them, yet I thought they were pleasant
to hear, for they were the first sound of a man's
voice that I had heard, my own excepted, for
above twenty-five years. But there was no time
for such reflections now; the savage who was
knocked down recovered himself so far as to sit
up upon the ground, and I perceived that my
savage began to be afraid; but when I saw that, I
presented my other piece at the man, as if I would

shoot him; upon this my savage, for so I call him now, made a motion to me to lend him my sword, which hung naked in a belt by my side; so I did: he no sooner had it, but he runs to his enemy, and at one blow cut off his head as cleverly, no executioner could have done it sooner or better; which I thought very strange, for one who I had reason to believe never saw a sword in his life before, except their own wooden swords; however, it seems, as I learned afterwards, they make their wooden swords so sharp, so heavy, and the wood is so hard, that they will cut off heads even with them, ay and arms, and that at one blow too; when he had done this, he comes laughing to me in sign of triumph, and brought me the sword again, and with abundance of gestures which I did not understand, laid it down with the head of the savage that he had killed, just before me.

But that which astonished him most, was to know how I had killed the other Indian so far off; so pointing to him, he made signs to me to let him go to him, so I bade him go, as well as I could; when he came to him, he stood like one amazed, looking at him, turned him first on one side, then on t'other, looked at the wound the bullet had made, which it seems was just in his breast, where it had made a hole, and no great quantity of blood had followed, but he had bled inwardly, for he was quite dead. He took up his bow and arrows, and came back, so I turned to go away, and beckoned to him to follow me, making signs to him that more might come after him.

Upon this he signed to me that he should bury them with sand, that they might not be seen by the rest if they followed; and so I made signs again to him to do so; he fell to work, and in an instant he had scraped a hole in the sand with his hands, big enough to bury the first in, and then dragged him into it, and covered him, and did so also by the other; I believe he had buried them both in a quarter of an hour; then calling him away, I took him not to my castle, but quite away to my cave, on the farther part of the island; so I did not let my dream come to pass in that part, that he came into my grove for shelter.

Here I gave him bread, and a bunch of raisins to eat, and a draught of water, which I found he was indeed in great distress for, by his running; and having refreshed him, I made signs for him to go lie down and sleep; pointing to a place where I had laid a great parcel of rice straw, and a blanket upon it, which I used to sleep upon myself sometimes; so the poor creature laid down, and went to sleep.

He was a comely handsome fellow, perfectly well made; with straight, strong limbs, not too large; tall and well shaped, and, as I reckon, about twenty-six years of age. He had a very good countenance, not a fierce and surly aspect; his hair was long and black, not curled like wool; his forehead very high and large, and a great vivacity and sparkling sharpness in his eyes. The colour of his skin was not quite black, but very tawny; his face was round and plump; his nose small, not flat like the negroes, a very good mouth, thin lips, and his fine teeth well set, and white as ivory. After he had slumbered, rather than slept, about half an hour, he waked again, and comes out of the cave to me; for I had been milking the goats, which I had in the enclosure just by; when he espied me, he came running to me, laying himself down again upon the ground, with all the possible signs of an humble thankful disposition, making many gestures to show it. At last he lays his head flat upon the ground, close to my foot, and sets my other foot upon his head, as he had done before; and after this, made all the signs to me of subjection, servitude, and submission imaginable, to let me know how he would serve me as long as he lived. I understood him in many things, and let him know I was very well pleased with him; in a little time I began to speak to him, and teach him to speak to me; and first, I made him know his name should be Friday, which was the day I saved his life; I called him so for the memory of the time; I likewise taught him to say Master, and then let him know that was to be my name; I likewise taught him to say yes and no, and to know the meaning of them; I gave him some milk in an earthen pot, and let him see me drink it before him, and sop my bread in it; and I gave him a cake of bread to do the like, which he quickly complied with, and made signs that it was very good for him.

I stayed there with him all that night; but as soon as it was day, I beckoned to him to come with me, and let him know I would give him some clothes, at which he seemed very glad, for he was stark naked. As we went by the place where he had buried the two men, he pointed exactly to the place, and showed me the marks that he had made to find them again, making signs to me that we should dig them up again, and eat them; at this I appeared very angry, expressed my abhorrence of it, made as if I would vomit at the thoughts of it, and beckoned with my hand to him to come away, which he did immediately, with great submission. I then led him up to the top of the hill, to see if his enemies were gone; and pulling out my glass, I looked, and saw plainly the place where they had been, but no appearance of them, or of their canoes; so that it was plain they were gone, and had left their two comrades behind them, without any search after them.

But I was not content with this discovery; but having now more courage, and consequently more curiosity, I took my man Friday with me, giving him the sword in his hand, with the bow and arrows at his back, which I found he could use very dextrously, making him carry one gun for me, and I two for myself, and away we marched to the place where these creatures had been; for I had a mind now to get some fuller intelligence of

them. When I came to the place, my very blood
ran chill in my veins, and my heart sank within
me, at the horror of the spectacle: indeed it was a
dreadful sight, at least it was so to me; though
Friday made nothing of it. The place was covered
with human bones, the ground dyed with their
blood, great pieces of flesh left here and there,
half eaten, mangled and scorched; and in short, all
the tokens of the triumphant feast they had been
making there, after a victory over their enemies. I
saw there skulls, five hands, and the bones of
three or four legs and feet, and abundance of
other parts of the bodies; and Friday, by his signs,
made me understand that they brought over four
prisoners to feast upon; that three of them were
eaten up, and that he, pointing to himself, was the
fourth; that there had been a great battle between
them and their next king, whose subjects it seems
he had been one of; and that they had taken a
great number of prisoners, all which were carried
to several places by those that had taken them in
the fight, in order to feast upon them, as was done
here by these wretches upon those they brought
hither.

I caused Friday to gather all the skulls, bones,
flesh, and whatever remained, and lay them together in a heap, and make a great fire upon it,
and burn them all to ashes: I found Friday had
still a hankering stomach after some of the flesh,
and was still a cannibal in his nature; but I showed
so much abhorrence at the very thought of it, and

at the least appearance of it, that he dared not
reveal it; for I had by some means let him know
that I would kill him if he offered it.

When we had done this, we came back to our
castle, and there I fell to work for my man Friday;
and first of all, I gave him a pair of linen drawers,
which I had found in the wreck; and which with a
little alteration fitted him very well; then I made
him a jerkin of goat's skin, as well as my skill
would allow; and I was now grown a tolerable
good tailor; and I gave him a cap, which I had
made of hare-skin, very convenient, and fashion-
able enough; and thus he was clothed for the
present, tolerably well, and was mighty well
pleased to see himself almost as well clothed as his
master. It is true, he went awkwardly in these
things at first; wearing the drawers was very awkward to him, and the sleeves of the waistcoat
galled his shoulders and the inside of his arms;
but a little easing them where he complained they
hurt him, and using himself to them, at length he
took to them very well.

The next day after I came home to my hutch
with him, I began to consider where I should
lodge him; and so that I might do well for him,
and yet be perfectly easy myself, I made a little
tent for him in the vacant place between my two
fortifications, in the inside of the last, and in the
outside of the first; and as there was a door or
entrance there into my cave, I made a formal door
frame, and a door to it of boards, and set it up in

the passage, a little within the entrance; and caus-
ing the door to open on the inside, I barred it up
in the night, taking in my ladders too; so that
Friday could no way come at me in the inside of
my innermost wall, without making so much noise
in getting over, that it must needs waken me; for
my first wall had now a complete roof over it; and
at the hole or place which was left to go in or out
by the ladder, I had placed a kind of trap-door,
which if it had been attempted on the outside,
would not have opened at all, but would have
fallen down and made a great noise; and as to
weapons, I took them all into my side every night.

But I needed none of all this precaution; for
never man had a more faithful, loving, sincere
servant, than Friday was to me; without passions, sullenness, or designs, perfectly obliged and
engaged; his very affections were tied to me,
like those of a child to a father; and I dare say
he would have sacrificed his life for the saving
mine upon any occasion whatsoever, the many
testimonies he gave me of this, put it out of
doubt, and soon convinced me that I needed to
use no precautions as to my safety on his account.

I was greatly delighted with my new companion,
and made it my business to teach him everything
that was proper to make him useful, handy, and
helpful; but especially to make him speak, and
understand me when I spoke, and he was the
aptest scholar that ever was, and particularly was
so merry, so constantly diligent, and so pleased,

when he could but understand me, or make me
understand him, that it was very pleasant to me to
talk to him; and now my life began to be so easy,
that I began to say to myself, that could I but
have been safe from more savages, I cared not if I
was never to remove from the place while I lived.

After I had been two or three days returned to
my castle, I thought that, in order to bring Friday
off from his horrid way of feeding, and from the
relish of a cannibal's stomach, I ought to let him
taste other flesh; so I took him out with me one
morning to the woods. I went in fact intending to
kill a kid out of my own flock, and bring him
home and dress it; but as I was going, I saw a she-
goat lying down in the shade, and two young kids
sitting by her. I caught hold of Friday. 'Hold,'
says I, 'stand still,' and made signs to him not to
stir; immediately I presented my piece, shot and
killed one of the kids. The poor creature, who had
at a distance seen me kill the savage his enemy,
but did not know or could imagine how it was
done, was visibly surprised, trembled and shook,
and looked so amazed that I thought he would
have sunk down. He did not see the kid I shot at,
or perceive I had killed it, but ripped up his
waistcoat to feel if he was not wounded, and as I
found, thought I was resolved to kill him; for he
came and kneeled down to me, and embracing my
knees, said a great many things I did not understand; but I could easily see that the meaning was
to pray me not to kill him.

I soon found a way to convince him that I would do him no harm, and taking him up by the hand, laughed at him, and pointed to the kid which I had killed, beckoned to him to run and fetch it, which he did; and while he was wondering and looking to see how the creature was killed, I loaded my gun again, and by and by I saw a great fowl like a hawk sit upon a tree within shot; so to let Friday understand a little what I would do, I called him to me again, pointed at the fowl, which was in fact a parrot, though I thought it was a hawk; I say, pointing to the parrot, and to my gun, and to the ground under the parrot, to let him see it would make it fall, I made him understand that I would shoot and kill that bird; I fired and bade him look, and immediately he saw the parrot fall, he stood like one frightened again, notwithstanding all I had said to him; and I found he was the more amazed because he did not see me put anything into the gun; but thought that there must be some wonderful fund of death and destruction in that thing, able to kill man, beast, bird, or anything near or far off, and the astonishment this created in him was such as could not wear off for a long time; and I believe, if I would have let him, he would have worshipped me and my gun. As for the gun itself, he would not so much as touch it for several days after; but would speak to it, and talk to it, as if it had answered him, when he was by himself; which, as I afterwards learned of him, was to desire it not to kill him.

Well, after his astonishment was a little over at this, I pointed to him to run and fetch the bird I had shot, which he did, but stayed some time; for the parrot, not being quite dead, had fluttered a good way off from the place where she fell; however, he found her, took her up, and brought her to me; and as I had perceived his ignorance about the gun before, I took this advantage to charge the gun again, and not let him see me do it, that I might be ready for any other mark that might present; but nothing more offered at that time; so I brought home the kid, and the same evening I took the skin off, and cut it out as well as I could; and having a pot for that purpose, I stewed some of the flesh, and made some very good broth; and after I had begun to eat some, I gave some to my man, who seemed very glad of it, and liked it very well; but that which was strangest to him was to see me eat salt with it; he made a sign to me that salt was not good to eat, and putting a little into his own mouth, he seemed to nauseate it, and would spit and sputter at it, washing his mouth with fresh water after it; on the other hand, I took some meat in my mouth without salt, and I pretended to spit and sputter for want of salt, as fast as he had done at the salt; but it would not do, he would never care for salt with his meat or in his broth; at least not a great while, and then but a very little.

Having thus fed him with boiled meat and broth, I was resolved to feast him the next day with roasting a piece of the kid; this I did by hanging it before the fire on a string, as I had seen many people do in England, setting two poles up, one on each side of the fire, and one across the top, and tying the string to the cross-stick, letting the meat turn continually. This Friday admired very much; but when he came to taste the flesh, he took so many ways to tell me how well he liked it, that I could not but understand him; and at last he told me he would never eat man's flesh any more, which I was very glad to hear.

The next day I set him to work at beating some corn out, and sifting it in the manner I used to do, as I observed before, and he soon understood how to do it as well as I, especially after he had seen what the meaning of it was, and that it was to make bread of; for after that I let him see me make my bread, and bake it too, and in a little time Friday was able to do all the work for me, as well as I could do it myself.

I began now to consider, that having two mouths to feed instead of one, I must provide more ground for my harvest, and plant a larger quantity of corn than I used to do; so I marked out a larger piece of land, and began the fence in the same manner as before, in which Friday not only worked very willingly and very hard, but did it very cheerfully, and I told him what it was for; that it was for corn to make more bread, because he was now with me, and that I might have enough for him and myself too. He appeared very aware of that part, and let me know that he thought I had much more labour upon me on his account than I had for myself; and that he would work the harder for me, if I would tell him what to do.

This was the pleasantest year of all the life I led in this place; Friday began to talk pretty well, and understand the names of almost everything I had occasion to call for, and of every place I had to send him to, and talked a great deal to me; so that, in short, I began now to have some use for my tongue again, which indeed I had very little occasion for before; that is to say, about speech; besides the pleasures of talking to him, I had a singular satisfaction in the fellow himself; his simple, unfeigned honesty appeared to me more and more every day, and I began really to love the creature; and on his side, I believe he loved me more than it was possible for him ever to love anything before.

I had a mind once to try if he had any hankering inclination to his own country again, and having taught him English so well that he could answer me almost any questions, I asked him whether the nation that he belonged to never conquered in battle; at which he smiled, and said, 'Yes, yes, we always fight the better'; that is, he meant always get the better in fight; and so we began the following discourse: 'You always fight the better,' said I; 'how came you to be taken prisoner then, Friday?'

*Friday*. My nation beat much, for all that.

*Master*. How beat? If your nation beat them, how came you to be taken?

*Friday*. They more many than my nation in the place where me was; they take one, two, three, and me; my nation over-beat them in the yonder place, where me no was; there my nation take one, two, great thousand.

*Master*. But why did not your side recover you from the hands of your enemies then?

*Friday*. They run one, two, three, and me, and make go in the canoe; my nation have no canoe that time.

*Master*. Well, Friday, and what does your nation do with the men they take, do they carry them away and eat them, as these did?

*Friday*. Yes, my nation eat mans too, eat all up.

*Master*. Where do they carry them?

*Friday*. Go to other place where they think.

*Master*. Do they come hither?

*Friday*. Yes, yes, they come hither; come other else place.

*Master*. Have you been here with them?

*Friday*. Yes, I been here. [*points to the NW side of the island, which, it seems, was their side*.]

By this I understood, that my man Friday had formerly been among the savages who used to come on shore on the farther part of the island, on the same man-eating occasions that he was now brought for; and some time after, when I took the courage to take him to that side, being the same I formerly mentioned, he immediately knew the place, and told me he was there once when they ate up twenty men, two women, and one child; he could not tell twenty in English; but he numbered them by laying so many stones in a row.

I have told this passage, because it introduces what follows; that after I had had this discourse with him, I asked him how far it was from our island to the shore, and whether the canoes were not often lost; he told me there was no danger, no canoes ever lost; but that after a little way out to the sea, there was a current, and wind, always one way in the morning, the other in the afternoon.

This I understood to be no more than the sets of the tide, as going out or coming in; but I afterwards understood it was occasioned by the great draught and reflux of the mighty river Oroonooko; in the mouth of which river, as I found afterwards, our island lay; and this land which I perceived to the west and north-west was the great island Trinidad, on the north point of the mouth of the river. I asked Friday a thousand questions about the country, the inhabitants, the sea, the coast, and what nations were near; he told me all he knew with the greatest openness imaginable; I asked him the name of the several nations of his sort of people; but could get no other name than Caribs from whence I easily understood that these were the Caribbees. He told me that up a great way beyond the moon, that was, beyond the setting of the moon, which must be west from their country, there dwelt white bearded men, like me; and pointed to my great whiskers, which I mentioned before; and that they had killed 'much mans', that was his word; by all which I understood, he meant the Spaniards, whose cruelties in America had been spread over the whole countries, and was remembered by all the nations from father to son.

I inquired if he could tell me how I might come from this island, and get among those white men; he told me, yes, yes, I might go 'in two canoe'; I could not understand what he meant, or make him describe to me what he meant by 'two canoe', till at last, with great difficulty, I found he meant it must be in a large boat, as big as two canoes.

This part of Friday's discourse began to relish with me very well, and from this time I entertained some hopes, that one time or other, I might find an opportunity to make my escape from this place; and that this poor savage might be a means to help me to do it.

After Friday and I became more intimately acquainted, and he could understand almost all I said to him, and speak fluently, though in broken English, to me, I acquainted him first, with true Christian religion, and then with my own story, or at least so much of it as related to my coming into the place, how I had lived there, and how long. I let him into the mystery, for such it was to him, of gunpowder and bullet, and taught him how to shoot; I gave him a knife, which he was wonderfully delighted with, and I made him a belt, with a frog for carrying a hatchet, which was not only as good a weapon in some cases, but much more useful upon other occasions.

I described to him the country of Europe, and particularly England, which I came from; how we lived, how we worshipped God, how we behaved to one another; and how we traded in ships to all parts of the world. I gave him an account of the wreck which I had been on board of, and showed him as near as I could the place where she lay; but she was all beaten in pieces before, and gone.

I showed him the ruins of our boat, which we lost when we escaped, and which I could not stir with my whole strength then, but was now fallen almost to pieces. Upon seeing this boat, Friday stood musing a great while, and said nothing; I asked him what it was he studied upon; at last says he, 'Me see such boat like come to place at my nation.'

I did not understand him a good while; but at last, when I had examined farther into it, I understood that a boat, such as that had been, came on shore upon the country where he lived; that is, as he explained it, was driven thither by stress of weather. I immediately imagined that some European ship must have been cast away upon their coast, and the boat might get loose, and drive ashore; but was so dull, that I never once thought of men making escape from a wreck thither, much less whence they might come; so I only inquired after a description of the boat.

Friday described the boat to me well enough; but brought me better to understand him, when he added with some warmth, 'We save the white mans from drown.' Then I presently asked him if there was any white mans, as he called them, in the boat. 'Yes,' he said, 'the boat full white mans.' I asked him how many; he told upon his fingers seventeen. I asked him then what became of them; he told me, 'They live, they dwell at my nation.'

This put new thoughts into my head; for I imagined that these might be the men belonging to the ship that was cast away in sight of my island, as I now call it; and who after the ship was struck on the rock, and they saw her inevitably lost, had saved themselves in their boat, and were landed upon that wild shore among the savages.

Upon this, I inquired of him more critically what was become of them. He assured me they lived still there; that they had been there about four years; that the savages let them alone, and gave them victuals to live. I asked him how it came to pass they did not kill them and eat them. He said, 'No, they make brother with them'; that is, as I understood him, a truce: and then he added, 'They no eat mans but when makes the war fight'; that is to say, they never eat any men but such as come to fight with them, and are taken in battle.

It was after this some considerable time, that

being upon the top of the hill, at the east side of
the island, from whence, as I have said, I had in a
clear day discovered the main or continent of
America; Friday, the weather being very serene,
looks very earnestly towards the mainland, and in
a kind of surprise, falls to jumping and dancing,
and calls out to me, for I was at some distance
from him. I asked him what was the matter. 'O
joy!' says he. 'O glad! There see my country,
there my nation!'

I observed an extraordinary sense of pleasure
appeared in his face, and his eyes sparkled, and
his countenance discovered a strange eagerness, as
if he had a mind to be in his own country again;
and this observation of mine put a great many
thoughts into me, which made me at first not so
easy about my new man Friday as I was before;
and I made no doubt but that if Friday could get
back to his own nation again, he would not only
forget all his religion, but all his obligation to me;
and would be forward enough to give his countrymen an account of me, and come back perhaps
with a hundred or two of them, and make a feast
upon me, at which he might be as merry as he
used to be with those of his enemies, when they
were taken in war.

But I wronged the poor honest creature very
much, for which I was very sorry afterwards.
However, as my jealousy increased and held me
some weeks, I was a little more circumspect, and
not so familiar and kind to him as before; in

which I was certainly in the wrong too, the honest, grateful creature having no thought about it, but what consisted with the best principles, both as a religious Christian, and as a grateful friend, as appeared afterwards to my full satisfaction.

While my jealousy of him lasted, you may be sure I was every day pumping him to see if he would reveal any of the new thoughts, which I suspected were in him; but I found everything he said was so honest and so innocent, that I could find nothing to nourish my suspicion; and in spite of all my uneasiness he made me at last entirely his own again, nor did he in the least perceive that I was uneasy, and therefore I could not suspect him of deceit.

## 11

One day walking up the same hill, but the weather being hazy at sea, so that we could not see the continent, I called to him, and said, 'Friday, do not you wish yourself in your own country, your own nation?' 'Yes,' he said, 'he be much O glad to be at his own nation.' 'What would you do there?' said I. 'Would you turn wild again, eat men's flesh again, and be a savage as you were before?' He looked full of concern, and shaking his head said, 'No, no, Friday tell them to live good, tell them to pray God, tell them to eat corn-bread, cattle-flesh, milk, no eat man again.' 'Why then,' said I to him, 'they will kill you.' He looked grave at that, and then said, 'No, they no kill me, they willing love learn.' He meant by this, they would be willing to learn. He added, they learned much of the bearded mans that come in the boat. Then I asked him if he would go back to them. He smiled at that, and told me he could not swim so far. I told him I would make a canoe for him. He told me he would go, if I would go with him. 'I go?' says I. 'Why, they will eat me if I come there.' 'No, no,' says he, 'me make they no eat

you; me make they much love you.' He meant he
would tell them how I had killed his enemies, and
saved his life, and so he would make them love
me; then he told me as well as he could, how kind
they were to seventeen white men, or bearded
men, as he called them, who came on shore there
in distress.

From this time I confess I had a mind to venture
over, and see if I could possibly join with these
bearded men, who I made no doubt were Spaniards or Portuguese; not doubting but if I could
we might find some method to escape from thence;
being upon the continent, and a good company
together; better than I could from an island forty
miles off the shore, and alone without help. So
after some days I told Friday I would give him a
boat to go back to his nation; and I took him to
my frigate which lay on the other side of the
island, and having cleared it of water, for I always
kept it sunk in the water, I brought it out, showed
it him, and we both went into it.

I found he was a most dextrous fellow at managing it, would make it go almost as swift and fast
again as I could; so when he was in, I said to him,
'Well, now, Friday, shall we go to your nation?'
He looked very dull at my saying so, which it
seems was because he thought the boat too small
to go so far. I told him we would go and make one
bigger and he should go home in it. He answered
not one word, but looked very grave and sad. I
asked him what was the matter with him. He

asked me thus, 'Why you angry mad with Friday, what me done?' I asked him what he meant; I told him I was not angry with him at all. 'No angry! No angry!' says he, repeating the words several times. 'Why send Friday home away to my nation?' 'Why', says I, 'Friday, did you not say you wished you were there?' 'Yes, yes,' says he, 'wish be both there, no wish Friday there, no master there.' In a word, he would not think of going there without me. 'I go there? Friday,' says I, 'what shall I do there?' He turned very quick upon me at this: 'You do great dcal much good,' says he, 'you teach wild mans be good sober tame mans; you tell them know God, pray God, and live new life.' 'Alas! Friday,' says I, 'thou knowest not what thou sayest, I am but an ignorant man myself.' 'Yes, yes,' says he, 'you teachee me good, you teachee them good.' 'No, no, Friday,' says I, 'you shall go without me, leave me here to live by myself, as I did before.' He looked confused again at that word, and running to one of the hatchets which he used to wear, he takes it up hastily, comes and gives it me. 'What must I do with this?' says I to him. 'You take, kill Friday,' says he. 'What must I kill you for?' said I again. He returns very quick, 'What you send Friday away for? Take, kill Friday, no send Friday away?' This he spoke so earnestly, that I saw tears in his eyes. In a word, I so plainly discovered the utmost affection in him to me, and a firm resolution in him, that I told him then, and often after, that I would never send him away from me, if he was willing to stay with me.

Upon the whole, as I found by all his discourse a settled affection to me, and that nothing should part him from me, so I found all the foundation of his desire to go to his own country was laid in his ardent affection to the people, and his hopes of my doing them good; a thing which as I had no notion of myself, so I had not the least thought or intention or desire of undertaking it. But still I found a strong inclination to my attempting an escape as above, founded on the supposition gathered from the discourse, that there were seventeen bearded men there; and therefore, without any more delay, I went to work with Friday to find out a great tree proper to fell, and make a large canoe to undertake the voyage. There were trees enough in the island to have built a little fleet, not of canoes, but even of good large vessels. But the main thing I looked at, was to get one so near the water that we might launch it when it was made.

At last, Friday pitched upon a tree, for I found he knew much better than I what kind of wood was fittest for it, nor can I tell to this day what wood to call the tree we cut down. Friday was for burning the hollow or cavity of this tree out to make it for a boat. But I showed him how rather to cut it out with tools, which, after I had showed him how to use, he did very handily, and in about a month's hard labour we finished it, and made it very handsome, especially when with our axes, which 1 showed him how to handle, we cut and hewed the outside into the true shape of a boat; after this, however, it cost us near a fortnight's time to get her along as it were inch by inch upon great rollers into the water. But when she was in, she would have carried twenty men with great ease.

When she was in the water, and though she was so big, it amazed me to see with what dexterity and how swift my man Friday would manage her, turn her, and paddle her along; so I asked him if he would, and if we might venture over in her. 'Yes,' he said, 'he venture over in her very well, though great blow wind.' However, I had a farther design that he knew nothing of, and that was to make a mast and sail and to fit her with an anchor and cable. As to a mast, that was easy enough to get; so I pitched upon a straight young cedar-tree, which I found near the place, and which there was great plenty of in the island, and I set Friday to work to cut it down, and gave him directions how to shape and order it. But as to the sail, that was my particular care; I knew I had old sails, or rather pieces of old sails enough; but as I had had them now six and twenty years by me, and had not been very careful to preserve them, not imagining that I should ever have this kind of use for them, I did not doubt that they were all rotten, and indeed most of them were so; however, I found two pieces which appeared pretty good, and with these I went to work, and with a great deal of pains, and awkward tedious stitching (you may be sure) for want of needles, I at length made a three-cornered ugly thing, like what we call in England a shoulder-of-mutton sail, to go with a boom at bottom, and a little short sprit at the top, such as usually our ships' longboats sail with, and such as I best knew how to manage; because it was such a one as I had on the boat in which I made my escape from Barbary, as related in the first part of my story.

I was near two months performing this last work of rigging and fitting my mast and sails; for I finished them very complete, making a small stay, and a sail or fore sail to it, to assist, if we should turn to windward; and which was more than all, I fixed a rudder to the stern of her, to steer with; and though I was but a bungling shipwright, yet as I knew the usefulness, and even necessity of such a thing, I applied myself with so much pains to do it, that at last I brought it to pass; though considering the many dull contrivances I had for it that failed, I think it cost me almost as much labour as making the boat.

After all this was done too, I had my man Friday to teach as to what belonged to the navigation of my boat; for though he knew very well how to paddle a canoe, he knew nothing what belonged to a sail and a rudder; and was the most amazed, when he saw me work the boat to and again in the sea by the rudder, and how the sail gybed, and filled this way or that way, as the course we sailed changed. However, with a little use, I made all these things familiar to him; and he became an expert sailor, except that as to the compass, I could make him understand very little of that. On the other hand, as there was very little cloudy weather, and seldom or never any fogs in those parts, there was the less occasion for a compass, seeing the stars were always to be seen by night, and the shore by day, except in the rainy seasons, and then nobody cared to stir abroad, either by land or sea.

I was now entered on the seven and twentieth year of my captivity in this place; though the last three years that I had this creature with me ought rather to be left out of the account, my habitation being quite of another kind than in all the rest of the time.

I now had an invincible impression upon my thoughts, that my deliverance was at hand, and that I should not be another year in this place. However, I went on with my husbandry, digging, planting, fencing, as usual; I gathered and cured my grapes, and did every necessary thing as before.

The rainy season was in the meantime upon me, when I kept more within doors than at other times; so I had stowed our new vessel as secure as we could, bringing her up into the creek, where as I said, in the beginning I landed my rafts from the ship, and hauling her up to the shore at high water mark, I made my man Friday dig a little dock, just big enough to hold her, and just deep enough to give her water enough to float in; and then when the tide was out, we made a strong dam across the end of it, to keep the water out; and so she lay dry, as to the tide from the sea; and to keep the rain off, we laid a great many boughs of trees, so thick that she was as well thatched as a house; and thus we waited for the month of November and December, in which I designed to make my adventure.

When the settled season began to come in, as the thought of my design returned with the fair weather, I was preparing daily for the voyage; and the first thing I did was to lay by a certain quantity of provisions, being the stores for our voyage; and intended, in a week or a fortnight's time, to open the dock and launch out our boat. I was busy one morning upon something of this kind, when I called to Friday, and bade him go to the sea-shore, and see if he could find a turtle or tortoise, a thing which we generally got once a week, for the sake of the eggs as well as the flesh. Friday had not been long gone, when he came running back, and flew over my outer wall, or fence, like one that felt not the ground, or the steps he set his feet on; and before I had time to speak to him, he cries out to me, 'O master! O master! O sorrow! O bad!' 'What's the matter, Friday?' says I. 'O yonder, there,' says he, 'one, two, three canoe! One, two, three!' By his way of speaking, I concluded there were six; but on inquiry, I found it was but three. 'Well, Friday,' says I, 'do not be frightened'; so I heartened him up as well as I could. However, I saw the poor fellow was most terribly scared; for nothing ran in his head but that they were come to look for him, and would cut him in pieces and eat him; and the poor fellow trembled so, that I scarce knew what to do with him. I comforted him as well as I could, and told him I was in as much danger as he, and that they would eat me as well as him; 'but,' says I, 'Friday, we must resolve to fight them; can you fight, Friday?' 'Me shoot,' says he, 'but there come many great number.' 'No matter for that,' said I again, 'our guns will frighten them that we do not kill'; so I asked him whether if I resolved to defend him, he would defend me, and stand by me, and do just as I bid him. He said, 'Me die, when you bid die, master'; so I went and fetched a good dram of rum, and gave him; for I had been so good a husband of my rum, that I had a great deal left. When he drank it, I made him take the two fowling-pieces, which we always carried, and load them with large swan-shot, as big as small pistol bullets; then I took four muskets, and loaded them with two slugs and five small bullets each; and my two pistols I loaded with a brace of bullets each; I hung my great sword as usual, naked by my side, and gave Friday his hatchet.

When I had thus prepared myself, I took my perspective-glass, and went up to the side of the hill, to see what I could discover; and I found quickly, by my glass, that there were one and twenty savages, three prisoners, and three canoes; and that their whole business seemed to be the triumphant banquet upon these three human bodies (a barbarous feast indeed), but nothing more than as I had observed was usual with them.

I observed also, that they were landed not where they had done when Friday made his escape, but nearer to my creek, where the shore was low, and where a thick wood came almost down to the sea. This, with the abhorrence of the inhuman errand these wretches came about, filled me with such indignation that I came down again to Friday, and told him I was resolved to go down to them, and kill them all; and asked him if he would stand by me. He had now got over his fright, and his spirits being a little raised with the dram I had given him, he was very cheerful, and told me as before, he would die, when I bid die.

In this fit of fury, I took first and divided the arms which I had charged, as before, between us; I gave Friday one pistol to stick in his girdle, and three guns upon his shoulder; and I took one pistol and the other three myself; and in this posture we marched out. I took a small bottle of rum in my pocket, and gave Friday a large bag, with more powder and bullet; and as to orders, I charged him to keep close behind me, and not to stir, or shoot, or do anything, till I bid him; and in the meantime, not to speak a word. In this posture I fetched a compass to my right hand, of near a mile, as well to get over the creek as to get into the wood; so that I might come within shot of them before I should be discovered, which I had seen by my glass it was easy to do.

While I was making this march, my former thoughts returning, I began to abate my resolution; I do not mean that I entertained any fear of their number; for as they were naked, unarmed wretches, 'tis certain I was superior to them; nay, though I had been alone; but it occurred to my thoughts, what call, what occasion, much less what necessity I was in to go and dip my hands in blood, to attack people who had neither done, or intended me any wrong.

These things were so warmly pressed upon my thoughts, all the way as I went, that I resolved I would only go and place myself near them, that I might observe their barbarous feast, and that I would act then as God should direct; but that unless something offered that was more a call to me than yet I knew of, I would not meddle with them.

With this resolution I entered the wood, and with all possible wariness and silence, Friday following close at my heels, I marched till I came to the skirt of the wood, on the side which was next to them; only that one corner of the wood lay between me and them; here I called softly to Friday, and showing him a great tree, which was just at the corner of the wood, I bade him go to the tree, and bring me word if he could see there plainly what they were doing; he did so, and came immediately back to me, and told me they might be plainly viewed there; that they were all about their fire, eating the flesh of one of their prisoners; and that another lay bound upon the sand, a little from them, which he said they would kill next, and which fired all the very soul within me; he told me it was not one of their nation, but one of the bearded men, who he had told me of, that came to their country in the boat. I was filled with horror at the very naming the white bearded man, and going to the tree, I saw plainly by my glass a white man who lay upon the beach of the sea, with his hands and his feet tied, and that he was an European, and had clothes on.

There was another tree, and a little thicket beyond it, about fifty yards nearer to them than the place where I was, which by going a little way about, I saw I might come at undiscovered, and that then I should be within range of them; so I withheld my passion, though I was indeed enraged to the highest degree, and going back about twenty paces, I got behind some bushes, which held all the way till I came to the other tree; and then I came to a little rising ground, which gave me a full view of them, at the distance of about eighty yards.

I had now not a moment to lose; for nineteen of the dreadful wretches sat upon the ground, all close huddled together, and had just sent the other two to butcher the poor Christian, and bring him perhaps limb by limb to their fire, and they were stooped down to untie the bands at his feet; I turned to Friday. 'Now, Friday,' said I, 'do as I bid thee'; Friday said he would; 'Then, Friday,' says I, 'do exactly as you see me do, fail in nothing'; so I set down one of the muskets and the fowling-piece upon the ground, and Friday did the like by his; and with the other musket I took my aim at the savages, bidding him do the like; then asking him if he was ready, he said yes. 'Then fire at them,' said I; and the same moment I fired also.

Friday took his aim so much better than I, that on the side that he shot, he killed two of them, and wounded three more; and on my side, I killed one, and wounded two. They were, you may be sure, in a dreadful consternation; and all of them, who were not hurt, jumped up upon their feet, but did not immediately know which way to run, or which way to look: for they knew not from whence their destruction came. Friday kept his eyes close upon me, that as I had bid him, he might observe what I did; so as soon as the first shot was made, I threw down the piece, and took up the fowling-piece, and Friday did the like; he sees me cock and present, he did the same again. 'Are you ready, Friday?' said I 'Yes,' says he; 'Let fly then,' says I, 'in the name of God,' and with that I fired again among the amazed wretches, and so did Friday; and as our pieces were now loaded with what I called swan-shot, or small pistol bullets, we found only two drop; but so many were wounded, that they run about yelling and screaming like mad creatures, all bloody, and miserably wounded, most of them; whereof three more fell quickly after, though not quite dead.

'Now, Friday,' says I, laying down the discharged pieces, and taking up the musket which was yet loaded, 'follow me,' says I; which he did, with a great deal of courage; upon which I rushed out of the wood, and showed myself, and Friday close at my foot; as soon as I perceived they saw me, I shouted as loud as I could, and bade Friday do so too; and running as fast as I could, which by the way, was not very fast, being laden with arms as I was, I made directly towards the poor victim, who was, as I said, lying upon the beach, between the place where they sat and the sea. The two butchers who were just going to work with him, had left him at the surprise of our first fire, and fled in a terrible fright to the sea-side, and had jumped into a canoe, and three more of the rest made the same way; I turned to Friday, and bid him step forwards, and fire at them; he understood me immediately, and running about forty yards to be near them, he shot at them, and I thought he had killed them all; for I see them all fall of a heap into the boat; though I saw two of them up again quickly: however, he killed two of them, and wounded the third; so that he lay down in the bottom of the boat, as if he had been dead.

While my man Friday fired at them, I pulled

out my knife, and cut the poor victim's bonds,
and loosing his hands and feet, I lifted him up,
and asked him in the Portuguese tongue what he
was. He answered in Latin, 'Christianus'; but was
so weak and faint, that he could scarce stand or
speak; I took my bottle out of my pocket, and
gave it him, making signs that he should drink,
which he did; and I gave him a piece of bread,
which he ate; then I asked him what countryman
he was, and he said, 'Espagniole'; and being a
little recovered, let me know by all the signs he
could possibly make, how much he was in my
debt for his deliverance. 'Seignior,' said I, with as
much Spanish as I could make up, 'we will talk
afterwards; but we must fight now; if you have
any strength left, take this pistol and sword, and
lay about you.' He took them very thankfully, and
no sooner had he the arms in his hands, but as if
they had put new vigour into him, he flew upon
his murderers like a fury, and had cut two of them
in pieces in an instant; for the truth is, as the
whole was a surprise to them, so the poor creatures
were so frightened with the noise of our pieces,
that they fell down for sheer amazement and fear;
and had no more power to attempt their own
escape, than their flesh had to resist our shot; and
that was the case of those five that Friday shot at
in the boat; for as three of them fell with the hurt
they received, so the other two fell with the fright.

I kept my piece in my hand still, without firing,
being willing to keep my charge ready, because I

had given the Spaniard my pistol and sword; so I called to Friday, and bade him run up to the tree from whence we first fired, and fetch the arms which lay there, that had been discharged, which he did with great swiftness; and then giving him my musket, I sat down myself to load all the rest again, and bade them come to me when they wanted. While I was loading these pieces, there happened a fierce engagement between the Spaniard and one of the savages, who made at him with one of their great wooden swords, the same weapon that was to have killed him before, if I had not prevented it. The Spaniard, who was as bold and as brave as could be imagined, though weak, had fought this Indian a good while, and had cut him two great wounds on his head; but the savage being a stout lusty fellow, closing in with him, had thrown him down (being faint) and was wringing my sword out of his hand, when the Spaniard, though undermost, wisely quitting the sword, drew the pistol from his girdle, shot the savage through the body, and killed him upon the spot, before I, who was running to help him, could come near him.

Friday, being now left to his liberty, pursued the flying wretches with no weapon in his hand but his hatchet; and with that he dispatched those three who, as I said before, were wounded at first and fallen, and all the rest he could come up with, and the Spaniard coming to me for a gun, I gave him one of the fowling-pieces with which he

pursued two of the savages, and wounded them
both; but as he was not able to run, they both got
from him into the wood, where Friday pursued
them, and killed one of them; but the other was
too nimble for him, and though he was wounded,
yet had plunged himself into the sea, and swam
with all his might off to those who were left in
the canoe, which three in the canoe, with one
wounded, who we know not whether he died or
no, were all that escaped our hands of one and
twenty.

Those that were in the canoe worked hard to
get out of range; and though Friday made two or
three shots at them, I did not find that he hit any
of them. Friday would fain have had me took one
of their canoes, and pursued them; and indeed I
was very anxious about their escape, lest carrying
the news home to their people, they should come
back perhaps with two or three hundred of their
canoes, and devour us by sheer multitude; so I
consented to pursue them by sea, and running to
one of their canoes, I jumped in, and bade Friday
follow me; but when I was in the canoe, I was
surprised to find another poor creature lying there
alive, bound hand and foot, as the spaniard was,
for the slaughter, and almost dead with fear, not
knowing what the matter was; for he had not been
able to look up over the side of the boat, he was
tied so hard, neck and heels, and had been tied so
long that he had really but little life in him.

I immediately cut his bonds and would have

helped him up; but he could not stand or speak, but groaned most piteously, believing it seems still that he was only unbound in order to be killed.

When Friday came to him, I bade him speak to him, and tell him of his deliverance, and pulling out my bottle, made him give the poor wretch a dram, which, with the news of his being delivered, revived him, and he sat up in the boat; but when Friday came to hear him speak, and look in his face, it would have moved anyone to tears, to have seen how Friday kissed him, embraced him, hugged him, cried, laughed, jumped about, danced, sung, and then cried again, wrung his hands, beat his own face and head, and then sang and jumped about again, like a distracted creature. It was a good while before I could make him speak to me, or tell me what was the matter; but when he came a little to himself, he told me that it was his father.

This action put an end to our pursuit of the canoe with the other savages, who were now almost out of sight; and it was happy for us that we did not; for it blew so hard within two hours after, and before they could have got a quarter of their way, and continued blowing so hard all night, and that from the north-west, which was against them, that I could not suppose their boat could live, or that they ever reached their own coast.

But to return to Friday, he was so busy about his father, that I could not find in my heart to take him off for some time: but after I thought he could leave him a little, I called him to me, and he came jumping and laughing, and pleased to the highest extreme; then I asked him if he had given his father any bread. He shook his head, and said, 'None: ugly dog eat all up self'; so I gave him a cake of bread out of a little pouch I carried on purpose; I also gave him a dram for himself, but he would not taste it, but carried it to his father. I had in my pocket also two or three bunches of my raisins, so I gave him a handful of them for his father. He had no sooner given his father these raisins, but I saw him come out of the boat, and run away, as if he had been bewitched, he ran at such a rate; for he was the swiftest fellow of his foot that ever I saw; I say, he ran at such a rate, that he was out of sight, as it were, in an instant; and though I called after him, it was all one, away he went, and in a quarter of an hour I saw him come back again, though not so fast as he went; and as he came nearer, I found his pace was slacker because he had something in his hand.

When he came up to me, I found he had been all the way home for an earthen jug to bring his father some fresh water, and that he had got two more cakes or loaves of bread: the bread he gave me, but the water he carried to his father: however, as I was very thirsty too, I took a little sup of it. This water revived his father more than all the rum or spirits I had given him; for he was just fainting with thirst.

When his father had drunk, I called to him to know if there was any water left; he said yes; and I bade him give it to the poor Spaniard, who was in as much want of it as his father; and I sent one of the cakes, that Friday brought, to the Spaniard too, who was indeed very weak, and was reposing himself upon a green place under the shade of a tree; and whose limbs were also very stiff, and very much swelled with the rude bandage he had been tied with. When I saw that upon Friday's coming to him with the water, he sat up and drank, and took the bread, and began to eat, I went to him and gave him a handful of raisins; he looked up in my face with all the tokens of gratitude and thankfulness that could appear in any countenance; but he was so weak, notwithstanding he had so exerted himself in the fight, that he could not stand up upon his feet; he tried to do it two or three times, but was really not able, his ankles were so swelled and so painful to him; so I bade him sit still, and caused Friday to rub his ankles, and bathe them with rum.

I observed the poor affectionate creature every two minutes, or perhaps less, all the while he was here, turned his head about, to see if his father was in the same place and posture as he left him sitting; and at last he found he was not to be seen; at which he started up, and without speaking a word, flew with that swiftness to him, that one could scarce perceive his feet to touch the ground as he went. But when he came, he only found he

had laid himself down to ease his limbs; so Friday
came back to me immediately, and I then spoke to
the Spaniard to let Friday help him up if he
could, and lead him to the boat, and then he
should carry him to our dwelling, where I would
take care of him. But Friday, a lusty strong fellow,
took the Spaniard up upon his back, and carried
him away to the boat, and set him down softly
upon the side of the canoe, with his feet in the
inside of it, and then lifted him quite in, and set
him close to his father, and immediately stepping
out again, launched the boat off, and paddled it
along the shore faster than I could walk, though
the wind blew pretty hard too; so he brought
them both safe into our creek; and leaving them in
the boat, runs away to fetch the other canoe. As
he passed me, I spoke to him, and asked him
whither he went; he told me, 'Go fetch more
boat'; so away he went like the wind; for sure
never man or horse ran like him, and he had the
other canoe in the creek, almost as soon as I got to
it by land; so he wafted me over, and then went to
help our new guests out of the boat, which he did;
but they were neither of them able to walk; so that
poor Friday knew not what to do.

To remedy this, I went to work in my thought,
and calling to Friday to bid them sit down on the
bank while he came to me, I soon made a kind of
hand-barrow to lay them on, and Friday and I
carried them up both together upon it between us.
But when we got them to the outside of our wall

or fortification, we were at a worse loss than
before; for it was impossible to get them over; and
I was resolved not to break it down: so I set to
work again; and Friday and I, in about two hours'
time, made a very handsome tent, covered with
old sails, and above that with boughs of trees,
being in the space without our outward fence, and
between that and the grove of young wood which
I had planted: and here we made them two beds
of such things as I had, with blankets laid upon it
to lie on, and another to cover them on each bed.

## 12

My island was now peopled, and I thought myself very rich in subjects; and it was a merry reflection which I frequently made, how like a king I looked. First of all, the whole country was my own property; so that I had an undoubted right of dominion. Secondly, my people were perfectly subjected: I was absolute lord and lawgiver; they all owed their lives to me, and were ready to lay down their lives, if there had been occasion of it, for me.

As soon as I had secured my two weak rescued prisoners, and given them shelter, and a place to rest them upon, I began to think of making some provision for them. And the first thing I did, I ordered Friday to take a yearling goat, betwixt a kid and a goat, out of my particular flock, to be killed, when I cut off the hinder quarter, and chopping it into small pieces, I set Friday to work to boiling and stewing, and made them a very good dish, I assure you, of flesh and broth, having put some barley and rice also into the broth; and as I cooked it without doors, for I made no fire within my inner wall, so I carried it all into the new tent; and having set a table there for them, I sat down and ate my own dinner also with them, and, as well as I could, cheered them and encouraged them; Friday being my interpreter, especially to his father, and indeed to the Spaniard too; for the Spaniard spoke the language of the savages pretty well.

After we had dined, or rather supped, I ordered Friday to take one of the canoes, and go and fetch our muskets and other firearms, which for want of time we had left upon the place of battle, and the next day I ordered him to go and bury the dead bodies of the savages, which lay open to the sun, and would presently be offensive; and I also ordered him to bury the horrid remains of their barbarous feast, which I knew were pretty much, and which I could not think of doing myself; nay, I could not bear to see them, if I went that way: all which he punctually performed, and defaced the very appearance of the savages being there; so that when I went again, I could scarce know where it was, otherwise than by the corner of the wood pointing to the place.

I then began to enter into a little conversation with my two new subjects; and first I set Friday to inquire of his father, what he thought of the escape of the savages in that canoe, and whether we might expect a return of them with a power too great for us to resist. His first opinion was, that the savages in the boat never could live out the storm, which blew that night they went off, but must of necessity be drowned or driven south to those other shores, where they were as sure to be devoured as they were to be drowned if they were cast away; but as to what they would do if they came safe on shore, he said he knew not; but it was his opinion that they were so dreadfully frightened with the manner of their being attacked, the noise and the fire, that he believed they would tell their people they were all killed by thunder and lightning, not by the hand of man, and that the two which appeared, Friday and me, were two heavenly spirits or furies, come down to destroy them, and not men with weapons. This he said he knew, because he heard them all cry out so in their language to one another, for it was impossible to them to conceive that a man could dart fire, and speak thunder, and kill at a distance without lifting up the hand, as was done now. And this old savage was in the right, for, as I understood since by other hands, the savages never attempted to go over to the island afterwards; they were so terrified with the accounts given by those four men (for it seems they did escape the sea), that they believed whoever went to that enchanted island would be destroyed with the fire from the gods.

This, however, I knew not, and therefore was under continual apprehensions for a good while, and kept always upon my guard, me and all my army; for as we were now four of us, I would have ventured upon a hundred of them fairly in the open field at any time.

In a little time, however, no more canoes appearing, the fear of their coming wore off, and I began to take my former thoughts of a voyage to the main into consideration, being likewise assured by Friday's father, that I might depend upon good usage from their nation on his account, if I would go.

But my thoughts were a little suspended when I had a serious discourse with the Spaniard, and when I understood that there were sixteen more of his countrymen and Portuguese, who having been cast away, and made their escape to that side, lived there at peace with the savages, but were very sore put to it for necessaries, and indeed for life. I asked him all the particulars of their voyage, and found they were a Spanish ship bound from the Rio de la Plata to the Havana, being directed to leave their loading there, which was chiefly hides and silver, and to bring back what European goods they could meet with there; that they had five Portuguese seamen on board, who they took out of another wreck; that five of their own men were drowned when the first ship was lost, and that these escaped through infinite dangers and hazards, and arrived almost starved on the cannibal coast, where they expected to have been devoured every moment.

He told me they had some arms with them, but they were perfectly useless, for that they had neither powder or ball, the washing of the sea having spoiled all their powder but a little, which they used at their first landing to provide themselves some food.

I asked him what he thought would become of them there, and if they had formed no design of making any escape. He said they had many consultations about it, but that having neither vessel, or tools to build one, or provisions of any kind, their councils always ended in tears and despair.

I asked him how he thought they would receive a proposal from me, which might tend towards an escape, and whether, if they were all here, it might not be done. I told him with freedom, I feared mostly their treachery and ill usage of me, if I put my life in their hands; I told him it would be very hard that I should be the instrument of their deliverance, and that they should afterwards make me their prisoner in New Spain; I added, that otherwise I was persuaded, if they were all here, we might, with so many hands, build a bark large enough to carry us all away, either to the Brasils southward, or to the islands or Spanish coast northward; but that if in requital they should, when I had put weapons into their hands, carry me by force among their own people, might be ill used for my kindness to them, and make my case worse than it was before.

He answered with a great deal of candour and ingenuity, that their condition was so miserable, and they were so sensible of it, that he believed they would abhor the thought of using any man unkindly that should contribute to their deliverance; and that, if I pleased, he would go to them with the old man, and discourse with them about it, and return again, and bring me their answer: that he would make conditions with them upon their solemn oath, that they should be absolutely under my leading, as their commander and captain, and that they should swear upon the holy sacraments and the Gospel, to be true to me, and to go to such Christian country as that I should agree to, and no other; and to be directed wholly and absolutely by my orders, till they were landed safely in such country as I intended; and that he would bring a contract from under their hands for that purpose.

Then he told me he would first swear to me himself that he would never stir from me as long as he lived, till I gave him orders; and that he would take my side to the last drop of his blood, if there should happen the least breach of faith among his countrymen.

He told me they were all of them very civil honest men, and they were under the greatest distress imaginable, having neither weapons or clothes, nor any food, but at the mercy and discretion of the savages; out of all hopes of ever returning to their own country; and that he was sure, if I would undertake their relief, they would live and die by me.

Upon these assurances, I resolved to venture to relieve them, if possible, and to send the old savage and this Spaniard over to them to negotiate.

But when we had all things in a readiness to go, the Spaniard himself started an objection, which had so much prudence in it on the one hand, and so much sincerity on the other hand, that I could not but be very well satisfied in it; and by his advice, put off the deliverance of his comrades for at least half a year. The case was thus:

He had been with us now about a month; during which time I had let him see in what manner I had provided, with the assistance of Providence, for my support; and he saw evidently what stock of corn and rice I had laid up; which as it was more than sufficient for myself, so it was not sufficient, at least without good husbandry, for my family, now it was increased to number four: but much less would it be sufficient, if his countrymen, who were, as he said, fourteen still alive, should come over. And least of all should it be sufficient to victual our vessel, if we should build one, for a voyage to any of the Christian colonies of America. So he told me, he thought it would be more advisable to let him and the two others dig and cultivate some more land, as much as I could spare seed to sow; and that we should wait another harvest, that we might have a supply of corn for his countrymen when they should come; for want might be a temptation to them to disagree, or not to think themselves delivered, otherwise than out of one difficulty into another.

His caution was so seasonable, and his advice so good, that I could not but be very well pleased with his proposal, as well as I was satisfied with his fidelity. So we fell to digging all four of us, as well as the wooden tools we were furnished with permitted; and in about a month's time, by the end of which it was seed time, we had gotten as much land cured and trimmed up, as we sowed twenty-two bushels of barley on, and sixteen jars of rice, which was in short all the seed we had to spare; nor in fact did we leave ourselves barley sufficient for our own food, for the six months that we had to expect our crop, that is to say, reckoning from the time we set our seed aside for sowing; for it is not to be supposed it is six months in the ground in that country.

Having now society enough, and our number being sufficient to put us out of fear of the savages, if they had come, unless their number had been very great, we went freely all over the island, wherever we found occasion; and as here we had our escape or deliverance upon our thoughts, it was impossible, at least for me, to have the means of it out of mine; to this purpose, I marked out several trees which I thought fit for our work, and I set Friday and his father to cutting them down; and then I caused the Spaniard, to whom I imparted my thought on that affair, to oversee and direct their work. I showed them with what indefatigable pains I had hewed a large tree into single planks, and I caused them to do the like, till they had made about a dozen large planks of good oak;

what prodigious labour it took up, anyone may imagine.

At the same time I contrived to increase my little flock of tame goats as much as I could; and to this purpose, I made Friday and the Spaniard go out one day, and myself with Friday the next day; for we took our turns: and by this means we got above twenty young kids to breed up with the rest; for whenever we shot the mother we saved the kids, and added them to our flock. But above all, the season for curing the grapes coming on, I caused a prodigious quantity to be hung up in the sun; and these with our bread was a great part of our food, and very good living too, I assure you; for it is an exceeding nourishing food.

It was now harvest, and our crop in good order; it was not the most plentiful increase I had seen in the island, but, however, it was enough to answer our end; for from our twenty-two bushels of barley we brought in and thrashed out above 220 bushels; and the like in proportion of the rice, which was store enough for our food to the next harvest, though all the sixteen Spaniards had been on shore with me; or if we had been ready for a voyage, it would very plentifully have victualled our ship, to have carried us to any part of the world, that is to say, of America.

When we had thus housed and secured our store of corn, we fell to work to make more baskets in which we kept it; and the Spaniard was very handy and dextrous at this part, and often blamed me that I did not make some things, for defence, of this kind of work; but I saw no need of it.

And now having a full supply of food for all the guests I expected, I gave the Spaniard leave to go over to the main, to see what he could do with those he had left behind him there. I gave him a strict charge in writing not to bring any man with him, who would not first swear in the presence of himself and of the old savage that he would no way injure, fight with, or attack the person he should find in the island, who was so kind to send for them in order to their deliverance; but that they would stand by and defend him against all such attempts, and wherever they went, would be entirely under and subjected to his commands; and that this should be put in writing, and signed with their hands. How we were to have this done, when I knew they had neither pen or ink, that indeed was a question which we never asked.

Under these instructions, the Spaniard and the old savage, the father of Friday, went away in one of the canoes, which they might be said to come in, or rather were brought in, when they came as prisoners to be devoured by the savages.

I gave each of them a musket, and about eight charges of powder and ball, charging them to be very good husbands of both, and not to use either of them but upon urgent occasion.

This was a cheerful work, being the first measures used by me in view of my deliverance for now twenty-seven years and some days. I gave them provisions of bread, and of dried grapes, sufficient for themselves for many days, and sufficient for all their countrymen for about eight days; and wishing them a good voyage, I saw them off, agreeing with them about a signal they should hang out at their return, by which I should know them again, when they came back, at a distance, before they came on shore.

They went away with a fair wind on the day that the moon was at full by my account, in the month of October: but as for an exact reckoning of days, after I had once lost it, I could never recover it again; nor had I kept even the number of years so punctually as to be sure that I was right, though as it proved, when I afterwards examined my account, I found I had kept a true reckoning of years.

## 13

It was no less than eight days I had waited for them, when a strange and unforeseen accident intervened, of which the like has not perhaps been heard of in history. I was fast asleep in my hutch one morning, when my man Friday came running in to me, and called aloud, 'Master, master, they are come, they are come.'

I jumped up, and regardless of danger, I went out, as soon as I could get my clothes on, and through my little grove, which by the way was by this time grown to be a very thick wood; I say, regardless of danger, I went without my arms, which was not my custom to do: but I was surprised, when turning my eyes to the sea, I presently saw a boat at about a league and a half's distance, standing in for the shore, with a shoulder-of-mutton sail, as they call it; and the wind blowing pretty fair to bring them in; also I observed that they did not come from that side which the shore lay on, but from the southernmost end of the island. Upon this I called Friday in, and bade him lie close, for these were not the people we looked for, and we might not know yet whether they were friends or enemies.

In the next place, I went in to fetch my perspective-glass, to see what I could make of them; and having taken the ladder out, I climbed up to the top of the hill, as I used to do when I was apprehensive of anything, and to take my view the plainer without being discovered.

I had scarce set my foot on the hill, when my eye plainly discovered a ship lying at anchor, at about two leagues and an half's distance from me south-south-east, but not above a league and a half from the shore. By my observation it appeared plainly to be an English ship, and the boat appeared to be an English longboat.

I cannot express the confusion I was in, though the joy of seeing a ship, and one which I had reason to believe was manned by my own countrymen, and consequently friends, was such as I cannot describe; but yet I had some secret doubts hung about me, I cannot tell from whence they came, bidding me keep upon my guard. In the first place, it occurred to me to consider what business an English ship could have in that part of the world, since it was not the way to or from any part of the world where the English had any traffic; and I knew there had been no storms to drive them in there, as in distress; and that if they were English really, it was most probable that they were here upon no good design; and that I had better continue as I was, than fall into the hands of thieves and murderers.

I had not kept myself long in this posture, but I saw the boat draw near the shore, as if they looked for a creek to thrust in at for the convenience of landing; however, as they did not come quite far enough, they did not see the little inlet where I formerly landed my rafts; but ran their boat on shore upon the beach, at about half a mile from me, which was very happy for me; for otherwise they would have landed just, as I may say, at my door, and would soon have beaten me out of my castle, and perhaps have plundered me of all I had.

When they were on shore I was fully satisfied that they were Englishmen. There were in all eleven men, whereof three of them I found were unarmed, and, as I thought, bound; and when the first four or five of them were jumped on shore, they took those three out of the boat as prisoners. One of the three I could perceive using the most passionate gestures of entreaty, affliction, and despair, even to a kind of extravagance; the other two I could perceive lifted up their hands sometimes, and appeared concerned indeed, but not to such a degree as the first.

I was perfectly confounded at the sight, and knew not what the meaning of it should be. Friday called out to me in English, as well as he could, 'O master! You see English mans eat prisoner as well as savage mans.' 'Why,' says I, 'Friday, do you think they are going to eat them then?' 'Yes,' says Friday, 'they will eat them.' 'No, no,' says I,

'Friday, I am afraid they will murder them indeed, but you may be sure they will not eat them.'

All this while I had no thought of what the matter really was, but stood trembling with the horror of the sight, expecting every moment when the three prisoners should be killed; nay, once I saw one of the villains lift up his arm with a great cutlass to strike one of the poor men; and I expected to see him fall every moment, at which all the blood in my body seemed to run chill in my veins.

I wished heartily now for my Spaniard, and the savage that was gone with him; or that I had any way to have come undiscovered within shot of them, that I might have rescued the three men; for I saw no fire-arms they had among them.

After I had observed the outrageous usage of the three men by the insolent seamen, I observed the fellows run scattering about the land, as if they wanted to see the country. I observed that the three other men had liberty to go also where they pleased; but they sat down all three upon the ground, very pensive, and looked like men in despair.

This put me in mind of the first time when I came on shore, and began to look about me; how I gave myself over for lost; how wildly I looked round me; what dreadful apprehensions I had; and how I lodged in the tree all night for fear of being devoured by wild beasts.

As I knew nothing that night of the supply I

was to receive by the providential driving of the ship nearer the land, by the storms and tide, by which I have since been so long nourished and supported; so these three poor desolate men knew nothing how certain of deliverance and supply they were, how near it was to them, and how effectually and really they were in a condition of safety, at the same time that they thought themselves lost, and their case desperate.

It was just at the top of high water when these people came on shore, and while partly they stood parleying with the prisoners they brought, and partly while they rambled about to see what kind of a place they were in, they had carelessly stayed till the tide was spent and the water was ebbed considerably away, leaving their boat aground.

They had left two men in the boat, who, as I found afterwards, having drunk a little too much brandy, fell asleep; however, one of them waking sooner than the other, and finding the boat too fast aground for him to stir it, called for the rest who were straggling about, upon which they all soon came to the boat; but it was past all their strength to launch her, the boat being very heavy, and the shore on that side being a soft sand, almost like a quicksand.

In this condition, like true seamen who are perhaps the least of all mankind given to forethought, they gave it over, and away they strolled about the country again; and I heard one of them say aloud to another, calling them off from the boat, 'Why, let her alone, Jack, can't ye, she will float next tide'; by which I was fully confirmed in the main inquiry, of what country they were.

All this while I kept myself very close, not once daring to stir out of my castle, any farther than to my place of observation, near the top of the hill; and very glad I was, to think how well it was fortified. I knew it was no less than ten hours before the boat could be floated again, and by that time it would be dark, and I might be at more liberty to see their motions, and to hear their discourse, if they had any.

In the meantime, I fitted myself up for a battle, as before; though with more caution, knowing I had to do with another kind of enemy than I had at first: I ordered Friday also, who I had made an excellent marksman with his gun, to load himself with arms: I took myself two fowling-pieces, and gave him three muskets. My figure indeed was very fierce; I had my formidable goat-skin coat on, with the great cap I have mentioned, a naked sword by my side, two pistols in my belt, and a gun upon each shoulder.

It was my design, as I said above, not to have made any attempt till it was dark: but about two o'clock, being the heat of the day, I found that in short they were all gone straggling into the woods, and, as I thought, were laid down to sleep. The three poor distressed men, too anxious for their condition to get any sleep, were however set down under the shelter of a great tree, at about a quarter of a mile from me, and, as I thought, out of sight of any of the rest.

Upon this I resolved to reveal myself to them, and learn something of their condition. Immediately I marched in the figure as above, my man Friday at a good distance behind me, as formidable for his arms as I, but not making quite so astonishing a spectre-like figure as I did.

I came as near them undiscovered as I could, and then, before any of them saw me, I called aloud to them in Spanish, 'What are ye, gentlemen?'

They started up at the noise, but were ten times more confounded when they saw me, and the uncouth figure that I made. They made no answer at all, but I thought I perceived them just going to fly from me, when I spoke to them in English: 'Gentlemen,' said I, 'do not be surprised at me; perhaps you may have a friend near you when you did not expect it.' 'He must be sent directly from heaven then,' said one of them very gravely to me, and pulling off his hat at the same time to me, 'for our condition is past the help of man.' 'All help is from heaven, sir,' said I. 'But can you put a stranger in the way how to help you, for you seem to me to be in some great distress? I saw you when you landed, and when you seemed to make applications to the brutes that came with you, I saw one of them lift up his sword to kill you.'

The poor man, with tears running down his face, and trembling, looking like one astonished, returned, 'Am I talking to god or man? Is it a real man, or an angel?' 'Be in no fear about that, sir,' said I, 'if God had sent an angel to relieve you, he would have come better clothed, and armed after another manner than you see me in; pray lay aside your fears, I am a man, an Englishman, and disposed to assist you, you see; I have one servant only; we have arms and ammunition; tell us freely, can we serve you? What is your case?'

'Our case,' said he, 'sir, is too long to tell you, while our murderers are so near; but in short, sir, I was commander of that ship, my men have mutinied against me; they have been hardly prevailed on not to murder me, and at last have set me on shore in this desolate place, with these two men with me, one my mate, the other a passenger, where we expected to perish, believing the place to be uninhabited, and know not yet what to think of it.'

'Where are those brutes, your enemies?' said I. 'Do you know where they are gone?' 'There they lie, sir,' said he, pointing to a thicket of trees; 'my heart trembles, for fear they have seen us, and heard you speak; if they have, they will certainly murder us all.'

'Have they any fire-arms?' said I. He answered they had only two pieces, and one which they left in the boat. 'Well then,' said I, 'leave the rest to me; I see they are all asleep, it is an easy thing to kill them all; but shall we rather take them prisoners?' He told me there were two desperate villains among them, that it was scarce safe to show any mercy to; but if they were secured, he believed all the rest would return to their duty. I asked him which they were. He told me he could not at that distance describe them; but he would obey my orders in anything I would direct. 'Well,' says I, 'let us retreat out of their view or hearing, lest they awake, and we will resolve further'; so they willingly went back with me, till the woods covered us from them.

'Look you, sir,' said I, 'if I venture upon your deliverance, are you willing to make two conditions with me?' He anticipated my proposals, by telling me that both he and the ship, if recovered, should be wholly directed and commanded by me in everything; and if the ship was not recovered, he would live and die with me in what part of the world soever I would send him; and the two other men said the same.

'Well,' says I, 'my conditions are but two. Firstly, that while you stay on this island with me, you will not pretend to any authority here; and if I put arms into your hands, you will upon all occasions give them up to me, and do no prejudice to me or mine upon this island, and in the meantime be governed by my orders.

'Secondly, that if the ship is or may be recovered, you will carry me and my man to England passage free.'

He gave me all the assurances that the invention and faith of man could devise, that he would comply with these most reasonable demands, and besides would owe his life to me, and acknowledge it upon all occasions as long as he lived.

'Well then,' said I, 'here are three muskets for you, with powder and ball; tell me next what you think is proper to be done.' He showed all the gratitude that he was able; but offered to be wholly guided by me. I told him I thought it was hard venturing anything; but the best method I could think of was to fire upon them at once, as they lay; and if any was not killed at the first volley, and offered to submit, we might save them, and so put it wholly upon God's providence to direct the shot.

He said very modestly, that he was loath to kill them, if he could help it, but that those two were incorrigible villains, and had been the authors of all the mutiny in the ship, and if they escaped, we should be undone still; for they would go on board, and bring the whole ship's company, and destroy us all. 'Well then,' says I, necessity legitimates my advice; for it is the only way to save our lives.' However, seeing him still cautious of shedding blood, I told him they should go themselves, and manage as they found convenient.

In the middle of this discourse, we heard some of them awake, and soon after we saw two of them on their feet. I asked him if either of them were of the men who he had said were the heads of the mutiny. He said, no. 'Well then,' said I, 'you may let them escape, and Providence seems to have wakened them on purpose to save themselves. Now,' says I, 'if the rest escape you, it is your fault.'

Animated with this, he took the musket I had given him in his hand and a pistol in his belt, and his two comrades with him, with each man a piece in his hand. The two men who were with him, going first, made some noise, at which one of the seamen who was awake turned about, and seeing them coming, cried out to the rest; but it was too late then; for the moment he cried out, they fired; I mean the two men, the captain wisely reserving his own piece. They had so well aimed their shot at the men they knew, that one of them was killed on the spot, and the other very much wounded; but not being dead, he started up upon his feet, and called eagerly for help to the other; but the captain stepping to him, told him, 'twas too late to cry for help, he should call upon God to forgive his villainy, and with that word knocked him down with the stock of his musket, so that he never spoke more. There were three more in the company, and one of them was also slightly wounded. By this time I was come, and when they saw their danger, and that it was in vain to resist, they begged for mercy. The captain told them he would spare their lives, if they would give him any assurance of their abhorrence of the treachery they had been guilty of, and would swear to be faithful to him in recovering the ship, and afterwards in carrying her back to Jamaica, from whence they came. They gave him all the protestations of their sincerity that could be desired, and he was willing to believe them, and spare their lives, which I was not against, only that I obliged him to keep them bound hand and foot while they were upon the island.

While this was doing, I sent Friday with the captain's mate to the boat, with orders to secure her and bring away the oars and sail, which they did; and by and by, three straggling men that were (happily for them) parted from the rest, came back upon hearing the guns fired, and seeing their captain, who before was their prisoner, now their conqueror, they submitted to be bound also; and so our victory was complete.

It now remained that the captain and I should inquire into one another's circumstances. I began first, and told him my whole history, which he heard with an attention even to amazement; and particularly at the wonderful manner of my being furnished with provisions and ammunition; and indeed, as my story is a whole collection of wonders, it affected him deeply; but when he reflected from thence upon himself, and how I seemed to have been preserved there on purpose to save his life, the tears ran down his face, and he could not speak a word more.

After this communication was at an end, I took him and his two men into my apartment, leading them in at the top of the house, where I refreshed them with such provisions as I had, and showed them all the contrivances I had made during my long, long inhabiting that place.

All I showed them, all I said to them, was perfectly amazing; but above all, the captain admired my fortification, and how perfectly I had concealed my retreat with a grove of trees, which having been now planted near twenty years, and the trees growing much faster than in England, was become a little wood, and so thick that it was unpassable in any part of it, but at that one side where I had reserved my little winding passage into it. I told him this was my castle and my residence, but that I had a seat in the country, as most princes have, whither I could retreat upon occasion, and I would show him that too another time; but at present our business was to consider how to recover the ship. He agreed with me as to that; but told me he was perfectly at a loss what measures to take; for there were still six and twenty hands on board, who having entered into a cursed conspiracy, by which they had all forfeited their lives to the law, would be hardened in it now by desperation; and would carry it on, knowing that if they were beaten, they should be brought to the gallows, as soon as they came to England, or to any of the English colonies; and that therefore there would be no attacking them with so small a number as we were.

I mused for some time upon what he had said, and found it was a very rational conclusion; and that therefore something was to be resolved on very speedily, as well to draw the men on board into some snare for their surprise, as to prevent their landing upon us, and destroying us; upon this it presently occurred to me, that in a little while the ship's crew, wondering what was become of their comrades and of the boat, would certainly come on shore in their other boat, to look for them, and that then perhaps they might come armed, and be too strong for us; this he allowed was rational.

Upon this, I told him the first thing we had to do was to stave the boat which lay upon the beach, so that they might not carry her off; and taking everything out of her, leave her so far useless as not to be fit to swim; accordingly we went on board, took the arms which were left on board out of her, and whatever else we found there, which was a bottle of brandy, and another of rum, a few biscuit cakes, a horn of powder, and a great lump of sugar in a piece of canvas; the sugar was five or six pounds; all which was very welcome to me, especially the brandy and sugar, of which I had had none left for many years.

When we had carried all these things on shore (the oars, mast, sail, and rudder of the boat were carried away before, as above) we knocked a great hole in her bottom, that if they had come strong enough to master us, yet they could not carry off the boat.

Indeed, it was not much in my thoughts that we could be able to recover the ship; but my view was that if they went away without the boat, I did not much doubt we could make her fit again, to carry us away to the Leeward Islands, and call upon our friends, the Spaniards, in my way, for I had them still in my thoughts.

While we were thus preparing our designs, and had first by main strength heaved the boat up upon the beach, so high that the tide would not float her off at high water; and besides, had broken a hole in her bottom, too big to be quickly stopped, and were sat down musing what we should do; we heard the ship fire a gun, and saw her hang out a flag, as a signal for the boat to come on board; but no boat stirred; and they fired several times, making other signals for the boat.

At last, when all their signals and firing proved fruitless, and they found the boat did not stir, we saw them, by the help of my glasses, hoist another boat out, and row towards the shore; and we found as they approached that there were no less than ten men in her, and that they had fire-arms with them.

As the ship lay almost two leagues from the shore, we had a full view of them as they came, and a plain sight of the men, even of their faces, because the tide having set them a little to the east of the other boat, they rowed up under shore, to come to the same place where the other had landed, and where the boat lay.

By this means, I say, we had a full view of them, and the captain knew the persons and characters of all the men in the boat, of whom he said that there were three very honest fellows, who he was sure were led into this conspiracy by the rest, being overpowered and frightened.

But that as for the boatswain, who it seems was the chief officer among them, and all the rest, they were as outrageous as any of the ship's crew, and were no doubt made desperate in their new enterprise, and terribly apprehensive he was that they would be too powerful for us.

I smiled at him, and told him that men in our circumstances were past the operation of fear: that seeing almost every condition that could be, was better than that which we were supposed to be in, we ought to expect that the consequence, whether death or life, would be sure to be a deliverance. I asked him what he thought of the circumstances of my life, and whether a deliverance were not worth venturing for. 'And where, sir,' said I, 'is your belief of my being preserved here on purpose to save your life, which elevated you a little while ago? For my part' said I, 'there seems to be but one thing amiss in all the prospect of it.' 'What's that?' says he. 'Why,' said I, ''tis that as you say, there are three or four honest fellows among them, which should be spared; had they been all of the wicked part of the crew, I should have thought God's providence had singled them out to deliver them into your hands; for depend upon it, every man of them that comes ashore are our own, and shall die or live as they behave to us.'

As I spoke this with a raised voice and cheerful countenance, I found it greatly encouraged him; so we set vigorously to our business. We had, upon the first appearance of the boat's coming from the ship, considered of separating our prisoners, and had indeed secured them effectually.

Two of them, of whom the captain was less assured than ordinary, I sent with Friday and one of the three delivered men to my cave, where they were remote enough, and out of danger of being heard or discovered, or of finding their way out of the woods, if they could have delivered themselves. Here they left them bound, but gave them provisions, and promised them if they continued there quietly, to give them their liberty in a day or two; but that if they attempted their escape, they should be put to death without mercy. They promised faithfully to bear their confinement with patience, and were very thankful that they had such good usage as to have provisions and a light left them; for Friday gave them candles (such as we made ourselves) for their comfort; and they did not know but that he stood sentinel over them at the entrance.

The other prisoners had better usage; two of them were kept pinioned indeed, because the captain was not free to trust them; but the other two were taken into my service upon their captain's recommendation, and upon their solemnly engaging to live and die with us; so with them and the three honest men, we were seven men, well armed;

and I had no doubt we should be able to deal well enough with the ten that were coming, considering that the captain had said there were three or four honest men among them also.

As soon as they got to the place where their other boat lay, they ran their boat in to the beach, and came all on shore, hauling the boat up after them, which I was glad to see; for I was afraid they would rather have left the boat at anchor, some distance from the shore, with some hands in her to guard her; and so we should not be able to seize the boat.

Being on shore, the first thing they did, they ran all to their other boat, and it was easy to see that they were under a great surprise, to find her stripped of all that was in her, and a great hole in her bottom.

After they had mused a while upon this, they set up two or three great shouts, calling with all their might, to try if they could make their companions hear; but all was to no purpose. Then they came all close in a ring, and fired a volley of their small-arms, which indeed we heard, and the echoes made the woods ring; but it was all one, those in the cave we were sure could not hear, and those in our keeping, though they heard it well enough, yet dared give no answer to them.

They were so astonished at this, that as they told us afterwards, they resolved to go all on board again to their ship, and let them know that the men were all murdered, and the longboat staved; accordingly they immediately launched their boat again, and got all of them on board.

The captain was terribly confounded at this, believing they would go on board the ship again, and set sail, giving their comrades for lost, and so he should still lose the ship, which he was in hopes we should have recovered; but he was quickly as much frightened the other way.

They had not been long put off with the boat, but we perceived them all coming on shore again; but with this new measure in their conduct, which it seems they consulted together upon, to leave three men in the boat, and the rest to go on shore, and go up into the country to look for their fellows.

This was a great disappointment to us; for now we were at a loss what to do; for our seizing those seven men on shore would be no advantage to us, if we let the boat escape; because they would then row away to the ship, and then the rest of them would be sure to set sail, and so our recovering the ship would be lost.

However, we had no remedy but to wait and see what the issue of things might present. The seven men came on shore, and the three who remained in the boat put her off to a good distance from the shore, and came to anchor to wait for them; so it was impossible for us to come at them in the boat.

Those that came on shore kept close together, marching towards the top of the little hill under which my habitation lay; and we could see them plainly, though they could not perceive us. We could have been very glad they would have come nearer to us, so that we might have fired at them, or that they would have gone farther off, that we might have come aboard.

But when they were come to the brow of the hill, where they could see a great way into the valleys and woods, which lay towards the northeast part, and where the island lay lowest, they shouted till they were weary; and not caring, it seems, to venture far from the shore, nor far from one another, they sat down together under a tree, to consider of it. Had they thought fit to have gone to sleep there, as the other party of them had done, they had done the job for us; but they were too full of apprehensions of danger to go to sleep, though they could not tell what the danger was they had to fear.

The captain made a very just proposal to me, upon this consultation of theirs, that perhaps they would all fire a volley again, to endeavour to make their fellows hear, and that we should all sally upon them, just at the juncture when their pieces were all discharged, and they would certainly yield, and we should have them without bloodshed. I liked the proposal, provided it was done while we were near enough to come up to them, before they could load their pieces again.

But this event did not happen, and we lay still a long time, very irresolute what course to take; at length I told them, there would be nothing to be done in my opinion till night, and then if they did not return to the boat, perhaps we might find a way to get between them and the shore, and so might use some stratagem with them in the boat to get them on shore.

We waited a great while, though very impatient for their removing; and were very uneasy, when after long consultations, we saw them start all up and march down toward the sea. It seems they had such dreadful apprehensions upon them of the danger of the place, that they resolved to go on board the ship again, give their companions over for lost, and so go on with their intended voyage with the ship.

As soon as I perceived them go towards the shore, I imagined it to be as it really was, that they had given over their search, and were for going back again; and the captain, as soon as I told him my thoughts, was ready to sink at the apprehensions of it; but I presently thought of a stratagem to fetch them back again, and which answered my end to a tittle.

I ordered Friday and the captain's mate to go over the little creek westward, towards the place where the savages came on shore when Friday was rescued; and as soon as they came to a little rising ground, at about half a mile distance, I bade them shout as loud as they could, and wait till they found the seamen heard them; that as soon as ever they heard the seamen answer them, they should return it again, and then keeping out of sight, take a round, always answering when the others called, to draw them as far into the island, and among the woods, as possible, and then wheel about again to me, by such ways as I directed them.

They were just going into the boat, when Friday and the mate called out, and they presently heard them, and answering, ran along the shore westward, towards the voice they heard, where they were presently stopped by the creek, where the water being up, they could not get over, and called for the boat to come up and set them over, as indeed I expected.

When they had set themselves over, I observed that the boat being gone a good way into the creek, and as it were, in a harbour within the land, they took one of the three men out of her to go along with them, and left only two in the boat, having fastened her to the stump of a little tree on the shore.

This was what I wished for, and immediately leaving Friday and the captain's mate to their business, I took the rest with me, and crossing the creek out of their sight, we surprised the two men before they were aware; one of them lying on shore, and the other being in the boat; the fellow on shore was between sleeping and waking, and going to start up; the captain, who was foremost, ran in upon him and knocked him down, and then called out to him in the boat, to yield, or he was a dead man.

There needed very few arguments to persuade a single man to yield, when he saw five men upon him, and his comrade knocked down; besides, this was, it seems, one of the three who were not so hearty in the mutiny as the rest of the crew, and therefore was easily persuaded, not only to yield, but afterwards to join very sincerely with us.

In the meantime, Friday and the captain's mate so well managed their business with the rest, that they drew them by calling and answering, from one hill to another, and from one wood to another, till they not only heartily tired them, but left them where they were very sure they could not reach back to the boat before it was dark; and indeed they were heartily tired themselves also by the time they came back to us.

We had nothing now to do but to watch for them in the dark, and to fall upon them, so as to make sure work with them.

## 14

It was several hours after Friday came back to me, before they came back to their boat; and we could hear the foremost of them long before they came quite up, calling to those behind to come along, and could also hear them answer and complain how lame and tired they were, and not able to come any faster, which was very welcome news to us.

At length they came up to the boat; but 'tis impossible to express their confusion, when they found the boat fast aground in the creek, the tide ebbed out, and their two men gone. We could hear them call to one another in a most lamentable manner, telling one another they were in an enchanted island; that either there were inhabitants in it, and they should all be murdered, or else there were devils and spirits in it, and they should be all carried away and devoured.

They shouted again, and called their two comrades by their names a great many times, but no answer. After some time, we could see them, by the little light there was, run about wringing their hands like men in despair; and that sometimes they would go and sit down in the boat to rest themselves, then come ashore again, and walk about again, and so over the same thing again.

My men would fain have me give them leave to fall upon them at once in the dark; but I was willing to take them at some advantage, so to spare them, and kill a few of them as I could; and especially I was unwilling to hazard the killing any of our own men, knowing the others were very well armed. I resolved to wait to see if they did not separate; and therefore to make sure of them, I drew my ambush nearer, and ordered Friday and the captain to creep upon their hands and feet as close to the ground as they could that they might not be discovered, and get as near them as they could possibly, before they offered to fire.

They had not been long in that posture, but that the boatswain, who was the principal ringleader of the mutiny, and had now shown himself the most dejected and dispirited of all the rest, came walking towards them with two more of their crew; the captain was so eager, as having this principal rogue so much in his power, that he could hardly have patience to let him come so near as to be sure of him; for they only heard his tongue before: but when they came nearer, the captain and Friday, starting up on their feet, let fly at them.

The boatswain was killed upon the spot, the next man was shot in the body and fell just by him, though he did not die till an hour or two after; and the third ran for it.

At the noise of the fire, I immediately advanced with my whole army, which was now eight men: myself *generalissimo*, Friday my lieutenant-general, the captain and his two men, and the three prisoners of war, who we had trusted with arms.

We came upon them in the dark, so that they could not see our number; and I made one of our men call to them by name, to try if I could bring them to a parley, and so might perhaps reduce them to terms, which fell out just as we desired: for indeed it was easy to think, as their condition then was, they would be very willing to capitulate; so he calls out as loud as he could, to one of them, 'Tom Smith, Tom Smith!' Tom Smith answered immediately, 'Who's that? Robinson?' for it seems he knew his voice. T'other answered, 'Ay, ay; for God's sake, Tom Smith, throw down your arms and yield, or you are all dead men this moment.'

'Who must we yield to? Where are they?' says Smith again. 'Here they are,' says he, 'here's our captain, and fifty men with him, have been hunting you this two hours; the boatswain is killed, Will Frye is wounded, and I am a prisoner; and if you do not yield, you are all lost.'

'Will they give us quarter then,' says Tom Smith, 'and we will yield?' 'I'll go and ask, if you promise to yield,' says Robinson; so he asked the captain, and the captain then calls himself out, 'You, Smith, you know my voice, if you lay down your arms immediately, and submit, you shall have your lives all but Will Atkins.'

Upon this, Will Atkins cried out, 'For God's sake, captain, give me quarter, what have I done? They have been all as bad as I'; which by the way was not true; for it seems this Will Atkins was the first man that laid hold of the captain, when they first mutinied, and used him barbarously, in tying his hands and giving him injurious language. However, the captain told him he must lay down his arms at discretion, and trust to the governor's mercy, by which he meant me; for they all called me governor.

In a word, they all laid down their arms, and begged their lives; and I sent the man that had parleyed with them, and two more, who bound them all; and then my great army of fifty men, which, particularly with those three, were all but eight, came up and seized upon them all, and upon their boat, only that I kept myself and one more out of sight, for reasons of state.

Our next work was to repair the boat, and think of seizing the ship; and as for the captain, now he had leisure to parley with them, he expostulated with them upon the villainy of their practices with him, and at length upon the farther wickedness of their design, and how certainly it must bring them to misery and distress in the end, and perhaps to the gallows.

They all appeared very penitent, and begged hard for their lives; as for that, he told them, they were none of his prisoners, but the commander's of the island; that they thought they had set him on shore in a barren uninhabited island, but it had pleased God so to direct them, that the island was inhabited, and that the governor was an Englishman; that he might hang them all there, if he pleased; but as he had given them all quarter, he supposed he would send them to England to be dealt with there as justice required, except Atkins, who he was commanded by the governor to advise to prepare for death; for he would be hanged in the morning.

Though this was all a fiction of his own, yet it had its desired effect; Atkins fell upon his knees to beg the captain to intercede with the governor for his life; and all the rest begged of him for God's sake, that they might not be sent to England.

It now occurred to me that the time of our deliverance was come, and that it would be a most easy thing to bring these fellows in to be hearty in getting possession of the ship; so I retired in the dark from them, that they might not see what kind of a governor they had, and called the captain to me; when I called, as at a good distance, one of the men was ordered to speak again, and say to the captain, 'Captain, the commander calls for you'; and presently the captain replied, 'Tell his Excellency, I am just coming.' This more perfectly deceived them; and they all believed that the commander was just by with his fifty men.

Upon the captain's coming to me, I told him my project for seizing the ship, which he liked wonderfully well, and resolved to put it in execution the next morning.

But in order to execute it with more art, and secure of success, I told him we must divide the prisoners, and that he should go and take Atkins and two more of the worst of them, and send them pinioned to the cave where the others lay: this was committed to Friday and the two men who came on shore with the captain.

They conveyed them to the cave, as to a prison; and it was indeed a dismal place, especially to men in their condition.

The others I ordered to my bower, as I called it, of which I have given a full description; and as it was fenced in, and they pinioned, the place was secure enough, considering they were upon their behaviour.

To these in the morning I sent the captain, who was to try them, and tell me whether he thought they might be trusted or no, to go on board and surprise the ship. He talked to them of the injury done him; of the condition they were brought to; and that though the governor had given them quarter for their lives as to the present action, yet that if they were sent to England, they would all be hanged in chains, to be sure; but that if they would join in so just an attempt as to recover the ship, he would have the governor's promise for their pardon.

Anyone may guess how readily such a proposal would be accepted by men in their condition; they fell down on their knees to the captain, and promised, with the deepest imprecations, that they would be faithful to him to the last drop, and that they should owe their lives to him, and would go with him all over the world, that they would own him for a father to them as long as they lived.

'Well,' says the captain, 'I must go and tell the governor what you say, and see what I can do to bring him to consent to it.' So he brought me an account of the temper he found them in; and that he verily believed they would be faithful.

However, that we might be very secure, I told him he should go back again, and choose out of those five and tell them, they might see that he did not want men, that he would take out those five to be his assistants, and that the governor would keep the other two, and the three that were sent prisoners to the castle (my cave), as hostages for the fidelity of those five; and that if they proved unfaithful in the execution, the five hostages should be hanged in chains alive upon the shore.

This looked severe, and convinced them that the governor was in earnest; however, they had no way left them but to accept it; and it was now the business of the prisoners, as much as of the captain, to persuade the other five to do their duty.

Our strength was now thus ordered for the expedition: Firstly, the captain, his mate, and passenger. Secondly, the two prisoners of the first gang, to whom, having their characters from the captain, I had given their liberty, and trusted them with arms. Thirdly, the other two who I had kept till now in my bower, pinioned; but upon the captain's motion, had now released. Fourthly, the five released at last: so that they were twelve in all, besides five we kept prisoners in the cave, for hostages.

I asked the captain if he was willing to venture with these hands on board the ship; for as for me and my man Friday, I did not think it was proper for us to stir, having seven men left behind; and it was employment enough for us to keep them asunder and supply them with victuals.

As to the five in the cave, I resolved to keep them fast, but Friday went in twice a day to them, to supply them with necessaries; and I made the other two carry provisions to a certain distance, where Friday was to take it.

When I showed myself to the two hostages, it was with the captain, who told them I was the person the governor had ordered to look after them, and that it was the governor's pleasure they should not stir anywhere, but by my direction; that if they did, they should be fetched into the castle, and be put in irons; so that as we never suffered them to see me as governor, so I now appeared as another person, and spoke of the governor, the garrison, the castle, and the like, upon all occasions.

The captain now had no difficulty before him, but to furnish his two boats, stop the breach of one, and man them. He made his passenger captain of one, with four other men; and himself, and his mate, and five more, went in the other: and they contrived their business very well; for they came up to the ship about midnight. As soon as they came within call of the ship, he made Robinson hail them, and tell them they had brought off the men and the boat, but that it was a long time before they had found them, and the like; holding them in a chat till they came to the ship's side; when the captain and the mate, entering first with their arms, immediately knocked down the second mate and carpenter with the butt-end of their muskets, being very faithfully seconded by their men; they secured all the rest that were upon the main and quarter decks, and began to fasten the hatches to keep them down who were below, when the other boat and their men, entering at the fore chains, secured the forecastle of the ship, and the scuttle which went down into the cook-room, making three men they found there prisoners.

When this was done, and all safe upon deck, the captain ordered the mate with three men to break into the round-house where the new rebel captain lay, who with two men and a boy had gotten fire-arms in their hands; and when the mate with a crow split open the door, the new captain and his men fired boldly among them, and wounded the mate with a musket ball, which broke his arm, and wounded two more of the men, but killed nobody.

The mate, calling for help, rushed however into the round-house, wounded as he was, and with his pistol shot the new captain through the head, the bullet entering at his mouth, and came out again behind one of his ears, so that he never spoke a word; upon which the rest yielded, and the ship was taken effectually, without any more lives lost.

As soon as the ship was thus secured, the captain ordered seven guns to be fired, which was the signal agreed upon with me, to give me notice of his success, which you may be sure I was very glad to hear, having sat watching upon the shore for it till near two o'clock in the morning.

Having thus heard the signal plainly, I laid me down; and it having been a day of great fatigue to me, I slept very sound, till I was surprised with the noise of a gun; and immediately starting up, I heard a man call me by the name of Governor, Governor, and I knew the captain's voice, when climbing up to the top of the hill, there he stood, and pointing to the ship, he embraced me in his arms. 'My dear friend and deliverer,' says he, 'there's your ship, for she is all yours, and so are we and all that belong to her.' I cast my eyes to the ship, and there she rode within little more than half a mile of the shore; for they had weighed her anchor as soon as they were masters of her; and the weather being fair, had brought her to anchor just against the mouth of the little creek; and the tide being up, the captain had brought the pinnace in near the place where I at first landed my rafts, and so landed just at my door.

I was at first ready to sink down with the surprise. For I saw my deliverance indeed visibly put into my hands, all things easy, and a large ship just ready to carry me away whither I pleased to go. At first, for some time, I was not able to answer him one word; but as he had taken me in his arms, I held fast by him, or I should have fallen to the ground.

He perceived the surprise, and immediately pulls a bottle out of his pocket, and gave me a dram of cordial, which he had brought on purpose for me; after I had drank it, I sat down upon the ground; and though it brought me to myself, yet it was a good while before I could speak a word to him.

All this while the poor man was in as great an ecstasy as I, and he said a thousand kind, tender things to me, to compose me and bring me to myself; but such was the flood of joy in my breast, that it put all my spirits into confusion; at last it broke out into tears, and in a little while I recovered my speech.

When we had talked awhile the captain told me he had brought me some little refreshment, such as the ship afforded, and such as the wretches that had been so long his master had not plundered him of. Upon this he called aloud to the boat, and bade his men bring the things ashore that were for the governor; and indeed it was a present, as if I had been one not that was to be carried away along with them, but as if I had been to dwell upon the island still, and they were to go without me.

First, he had brought me a case of bottles full of excellent cordial waters, six large bottles of Madeira wine; the bottles held two quarts apiece; two pound of excellent good tobacco, twelve good pieces of the ship's beef, and six pieces of pork, with a bag full of lemons, and two bottles of lime juice, and abundance of other things. But besides these, and what was a thousand times more useful to me, he brought me six clean new shirts, six very good neck-clothes, two pair of gloves, one pair of shoes, a hat, and one pair of stockings, and a very good suit of clothes of his own, which had been worn but very little: in a word he clothed me from head to foot.

It was a very kind and agreeable present, as anyone may imagine to one in my circumstances: but never was anything in the world of that kind so unpleasant, awkward, and uneasy, as it was to me to wear such clothes at their first putting on.

After these ceremonies, and after all his good things were brought into my little apartment, we began to consult what was to be done with the prisoners we had; for it was worth considering, whether we might venture to take them away with us or no, especially two of them, who we knew to be incorrigible and refractory to the last degree; and the captain said, he knew they were such rogues, that there was no obliging them, and if he did carry them away, it must be done in irons, as malefactors to be delivered over to justice at the first English colony he could come at; and I found that the captain himself was very anxious about it.

Upon this, I told him that if he desired it, I undertook to bring the two men he spoke of, to make it their own request that he should leave them upon the island. 'I should be very glad of that,' says the captain, 'with all my heart.'

'Well,' says I, 'I will send for them, and talk with them for you'; so I caused Friday and the two hostages, for they were now discharged, their comrades having performed their promise; I say, I caused them to go to the cave, and bring up the five men pinioned, as they were, to the bower, and keep them there till I came.

After some time, I came thither dressed in my new habit, and now I was called governor again; being all met, and the captain with me, I caused the men to be brought before me, and I told them I had had a full account of their villainous behaviour to the captain, and how they had run away with the ship, and were preparing to commit farther robberies, but that Providence had ensnared them in their own ways, and that they were fallen into the pit which they had dug for others.

I let them know that by my direction the ship had been seized, that she lay now in the bay; and they might see by and by that their new captain had received the reward of his villainy; for they might see him hanging at the yard-arm.

That as to them, I wanted to know what they had to say, why I should not execute them as pirates taken in the fact, as by my commission they could not doubt I had authority to do.

One of them answered in the name of the rest, that they had nothing to say but this, that when they were taken, the captain promised them their lives, and they humbly implored my mercy; but I told them I knew not what mercy to show them; for as for myself, I had resolved to quit the island with all my men, and had taken passage with the captain to go for England; and as for the captain, he could not carry them to England, other than as prisoners in irons to be tried for mutiny and running away with the ship; the consequence of which, they must needs know, would be the gallows; so that I could not tell which was best for them, unless they had a mind to take their fate in the island; if they desired that, I had some inclination to give them their lives, if they thought they could shift on shore.

They seemed very thankful for it, said they would much rather venture to stay there, than to be carried to England to be hanged, so I left it on that issue.

However, the captain seemed to make some difficulty of it, as if he dared not leave them there. Upon this I seemed a little angry with the captain, and told him that they were my prisoners, not his; and that seeing I had offered them so much favour, I would be as good as my word; and that if he did not think fit to consent to it, I would set them at liberty, as I found them; and if he did not like it, he might take them again if he could catch them.

Upon this they appeared very thankful, and I accordingly set them at liberty, and bade them retire into the woods to the place whence they came, as I would leave them some fire-arms, some ammunition, and some directions how they should live very well, if they thought fit.

Upon this I prepared to go on board the ship, but told the captain that I would stay that night to prepare my things, and desired him to go on board in the meantime, and keep all right in the ship, and send the boat on shore the next day for me; ordering him in the meantime to cause the new captain who was killed to be hanged at the yard-arm that these men might see him.

When the captain was gone, I sent for the men up to me to my apartment, and entered seriously into discourse with them of their circumstances; I told them I thought they had made a right choice; that if the captain carried them away, they would certainly be hanged. I showed them the new captain hanging at the yard-arm of the ship, and told them they had nothing less to expect.

When they had all declared their willingness to stay, I then told them I would let them into the story of my living there, and put them into the way of making it easy to them. Accordingly I gave them the whole history of the place, and of my coming to it, showed them my fortifications, the way I made my bread, planted my corn, cured my grapes; and in a word, all that was necessary to make them easy. I told them the story also of the sixteen Spaniards that were to be expected; for whom I left a letter, and made them promise to treat them in common with themselves.

I left them my fire-arms, and three swords. I had above a barrel and half of powder left; for after the first year or two, I used but little, and wasted none. I gave them a description of the way I managed the goats, and directions to milk and fatten them, and to make both butter and cheese.

In a word, I gave them every part of my own story; and I told them I would prevail with the captain to leave them two barrels of gunpowder more, and some garden seeds, which I told them I would have been very glad of; also I gave them the bag of peas which the captain had brought me to eat, and bade them be sure to sow and increase them.

Having done all this, I left them the next day, and went on board the ship: we prepared immediately to sail, but did not weigh that night. The next morning early, two of the five men came swimming to the ship's side, and making a most lamentable complaint of the other three, begged to be taken into the ship, for God's sake, for they should be murdered, and begged the captain to take them on board, even if he hanged them immediately.

Upon this the captain pretended to have no power without me; but after some difficulty, and after their solemn promises of amendment, they were taken on board, and were some time after soundly whipped and pickled; after which, they proved very honest and quiet fellows.

Some time after this, the boat was ordered on shore, the tide being up, with the things promised to the men, to which the captain at my intercession caused their chests and clothes to be added, which they took, and were very thankful for; I also encouraged them, by telling them that if it lay in my way to send any vessel to take them in, I would not forget them.

When I took leave of this island, I carried on board for souvenirs the great goat's skin cap I had made, my umbrella, and my parrot; also I forgot not to take the money I formerly mentioned, which had lain by me so long useless, that it was grown rusty or tarnished, and could hardly pass for silver till it had been a little rubbed and handled; as also the money I found in the wreck of the Spanish ship.

And thus I left the island, the nineteenth of December as I found by the ship's account, in the year 1686, after I had been upon it eight and twenty years, two months, and nineteen days; being delivered from this second captivity the same day of the month that I first made my escape in the barco-longo, from among the Moors of Sallee.

In this vessel, after a long voyage, I arrived in England, the eleventh of June, in the year 1687, having been thirty and five years absent.

# EPILOGUE

When I came to England, I was as perfect a stranger to all the world, as if I had never been known there. My benefactor and faithful steward, who I had left in trust with my money, was alive, but had had great misfortunes in the world; was become a widow the second time, and very low in the world. I made her easy as to what she owed me, assuring her I would give her no trouble; but on the contrary, in gratitude to her former care and faithfulness to me, relieved her as my little stock would afford, which at that time would indeed allow me to do but little for her; but I assured her I would never forget her former kindness to me.

I went down afterwards into Yorkshire; but my father was dead, and my mother, and all the family extinct, except that I found two sisters, and two of the children of one of my brothers; and as I had been long ago given over for dead, there had been no provision made for me; so that in a word, I found nothing to relieve or assist me; and that little money I had, would not do much for me, as to settling in the world.

I met with one piece of gratitude indeed, which I did not expect; and this was that the master of the ship, who I had so happily delivered, and by the same means saved the ship and cargo, having given a very handsome account to the owners of the manner how I had saved the lives of the men, and the ship, they invited me to meet them and some other merchants concerned, and altogether made me a very handsome compliment upon the subject, and a present of almost two hundred pounds sterling.

But after making several reflections upon the circumstances of my life, and how little way this would go towards settling me in the world, I resolved to go to Lisbon, and see if I might not come by some information of the state of my plantation in the Brasils, and of what was become of my partner, who I had reason to suppose had some years now given me over for dead.

With this view I took shipping for Lisbon, where I arrived in April following; my man Friday accompanying me very honestly in all these ramblings, and proving a most faithful servant upon all occasions.

When I came to Lisbon I found out by inquiry, and to my particular satisfaction, my old friend the captain of the ship, who first took me up at sea, off the shore of Africa. He was now grown old, and had left off the sea, having put his son, who was far from a young man, into his ship, and who still used the Brasil trade. The old man did not know me, and indeed, I hardly knew him; but I soon brought him to my remembrance, and as soon brought myself to his remembrance, when I told him who I was.

After some passionate expressions of the old acquaintance, I inquired, you may be sure, after my plantation and my partner. The old man told me he had not been in the Brasils for about nine years; but that he could assure me, that when he came away my partner was living, but the trustees, who I had joined with him to take cognizance of my part, were both dead; that, however, he believed that I would have a very good account of the improvement of the plantation; for that upon the general belief of my being cast away and drowned, my trustees had given in the account of the produce of my part of the plantation, to the procurator fiscal, who had appropriated it, in case I never came to claim it; one third to the king, and two thirds to the monastery of St Augustine, to be expended for the benefit of the poor, and for the conversion of the Indians to the Catholic faith; but that if I appeared, or anyone for me, to claim the inheritance, it should be restored; only that the improvement, or annual production, being distributed to charitable uses, could not be restored; but he assured me, that the steward of the king's revenue (from lands) and the steward of the monastery, had taken great care all along, that the incumbent, that is to say my partner, gave every year a faithful account of the produce, of which they received duly my portion.

I remained in Lisbon to settle my affairs. Within

seven months, I received what I was owed from the survivors of the trustees; the merchants for whose account I had gone to sea.

I was now master, all on a sudden, of above £5,000 sterling in money, and had an estate, as I might well call it, in the Brasils, of above a thousand pounds a year, as sure as an estate of lands in England: and in a word, I was in a condition which I scarce knew how to understand, or how to compose myself for the enjoyment of it.

My interest in the Brasils seemed to summon me thither; but now I could not tell how to think of going thither, till I had settled my affairs, and left my effects in some safe hands behind me. At first I thought of my old friend the widow, who I knew was honest and would be just to me, but then she was in years, and but poor, and, for ought I knew, might be in debt; so that in a word, I had no way but to go back to England myself, and take my effects with me.

I arrived in London in January of the next year and began to think of leaving my effects with the good widow, and setting out for Lisbon, and so to the Brasils. However, my true friend, the widow, earnestly dissuaded me from it, and so far prevailed with me, that I sold my estate in the Brasils for £20,000, and for almost seven years she prevented my running abroad; during which time I took my two nephews, the children of one of my brothers, into my care. The eldest having something of his own, I bred up as a gentleman, and gave him a settlement of some addition to his estate, after my decease; the other I put out to a captain of a ship; and after five years, finding him a sensible, bold, enterprising young fellow, I put him into a good ship, and sent him to sea: and this young fellow afterwards drew me in, as old as I was, to farther adventures myself.

In the meantime I in part settled myself here; for first of all I married, and that not either to my disadvantage or dissatisfaction, and had three children, two sons and one daughter: but my wife dying, and my nephew coming home with good success from a voyage to Spain, my inclination to go abroad, and his importunity, prevailed and engaged me to go in his ship, as a private trader to the East Indies. This was in the year 1694.

In this voyage I visited my new colony in the island, saw my successors the Spaniards, had the whole story of their lives, and of the villains I left there; how at first they insulted the poor Spaniards, how they afterwards agreed, disagreed, united, separated, and how at last the Spaniards were obliged to use violence with them, how they were subjected to the Spaniards, how honestly the Spaniards used them; a history, if it were entered into, as full of variety and wonderful accidents as my own part; particularly also as to their battles with the Caribbeans, who landed several times upon the island, and as to the improvement they made upon the island itself, and how five of them made an attempt upon the mainland, and brought away eleven men and five women prisoners, by which, at my coming, I found about twenty young children on the island.

Here I stayed about twenty days, left them supplies of all necessary things, and particularly of arms, powder, shot, clothes, tools, and two workmen, which I brought from England with me, a carpenter and a smith.

Besides this, I shared the island into parts with them, reserved to myself the property of the whole, but gave them such parts respectively as they agreed on; and having settled all things with them, and engaged them not to leave the place, I left them there.

From thence I touched at the Brasils, from whence I sent a bark, which I bought there, with more people to the island, and in it, besides other supplies, I sent seven women, being such as I found proper for service, or for wives to such as would take them. As to the Englishmen, I promised them to send them some women from England, with a good cargo of necessaries, if they would apply themselves to planting, which I afterwards performed. And the fellows proved very honest and diligent after they were mastered and had their properties set apart for them. I sent them also from the Brasils five cows, three of them being big with calf, some sheep, and some hogs, which, when I came again, were considerably increased.

But all these things, with an account how three

hundred Caribees came and invaded them, and ruined their plantations, and how they fought with that whole number twice, and were at first defeated, and three of them killed; but at last a storm destroying their enemies' canoes, they famished or destroyed almost all the rest, and renewed and recovered the possession of their plantation, and still lived upon the island; all these things, with some very surprising incidents in some new adventures of my own, for ten years more, I may perhaps give a farther account of hereafter.

## AT THE BACK OF THE NORTH WIND
*George MacDonald*

One night the North Wind comes into the hayloft where Diamond sleeps, and takes him flying with her. It is the start of many adventures for the coachman's son, with hardships to face and challenges to master by day, and his strange, beautiful and sometimes terrible journeys by night, before at last he reaches the country at the back of the North Wind.

## THE CALL OF THE WILD
*Jack London*

Buck is a dog born to luxury, but betrayed and sold to be a sledge dog in the harsh and frozen Yukon. This is the remarkable story of how Buck rises above his enemies to become one of the most feared and admired dogs in the north.

## THE CORAL ISLAND
*R. M. Ballantyne*

Fifteen-year-old Ralph, mischievous young
Peterkin and clever, brave Jack are shipwrecked on
a coral reef with only a telescope and a broken
penknife between them. At first the island seems a
paradise, with its plentiful foods and wealth of
natural wonders. But then a party of cannibals
arrives, and after that a pirate ship . . .

## THE COUNT OF MONTE CRISTO
*Alexandre Dumas*

Young Edmond Dantes has everything to look
forward to – he is soon to be captain of his own
ship and to marry his beloved Mercedes. But his
future is cruelly blighted when spiteful enemies
provoke his wrongful arrest and he is condemned
to lifelong imprisonment. Dantes' fate seems
sealed. How can he avenge his accusers and
reverse his fortune? The answer lies hidden on the
Island of Monte Cristo . . .

## GREAT EXPECTATIONS
*Charles Dickens*

As a small boy at Joe Gargery's forge, Pip meets
two people who will affect his whole life – an
escaped convict, Magwitch, he is forced to help,
and the eccentric Miss Havisham, whose beautiful,
cold ward Estella young Pip adores. But when a
secret benefactor pays for him to go to London to
become a gentleman, Pip never dreams he will
meet the dreadful Magwitch again, nor just how
wrong his expectations are . . .

## GULLIVER'S TRAVELS
*Jonathan Swift*

Gulliver sees life from many different perspectives
during the course of his exciting voyages around
the world. In Lilliput he is a giant among a race of
little people only six inches high; in Brobdingnag,
he himself seems tiny compared to the giant
inhabitants; and in the country of the
Houyhnhnms, horses rule and the human
creatures there have the status of animals. Life
back in England seems very ordinary after all that
he has seen.

## THE HOUND OF THE BASKERVILLES
*Sir Arthur Conan Doyle*

When Sir Charles Baskerville is found mysteriously dead in the grounds of Baskerville Hall, everyone remembers the legend of the monstrous creature that haunts the moor. The greatest detective in the world, Sherlock Holmes knows there must be a more rational explanation – but the difficulty is to find it before the hellhound finds him.

## THE HUNCHBACK OF NOTRE-DAME
*Victor Hugo*

Outcast by society because of his hideous appearance, Quasimodo lives under the protection of Claude Frollo, his foster father, and the cathedral itself. His world revolves around his fifteen bells and Frollo. But once the beautiful gypsy girl, La Esmerelda, enters their lives, all begins to crumble and things can never return to the way they were.

## JOURNEY TO THE CENTRE OF THE EARTH
*Jules Verne*

When Axel deciphers an old parchment that describes a secret passage through a volcano to the centre of the earth, nothing will stop his eccentric Uncle Lidenbrock from setting out at once. So, with silent Hans the guide, the two men embark on a perilous, astonishing, terrifying journey through the subterranean world – the most incredible voyage ever.

## KIDNAPPED
*Robert Louis Stevenson*

Young David Balfour came to the sinister House of Shaws to claim his inheritance. Instead, he found himself kidnapped.

With the help of daring rebel Alan Breck, David escapes, only to get mixed up in a desperate adventure – suspected of murder himself, and hunted across the Scottish moors.

### THE LOST WORLD
*Sir Arthur Conan Doyle*

To prove himself to the woman he wants to marry, journalist Ed Malone asks for a mission with 'adventure and danger in it'. And although his editor only sends him to interview touchy Professor Challenger, Ed gets more of both than he bargained for. Challenger leads him to a hidden plateau in the South American jungle – a world of carnivorous dinosaurs, giant fish-lizards and murderous ape-men ...

### THE PHANTOM OF THE OPERA
*Gaston Leroux*

The legendary rumours of an 'opera ghost' take on a terrifying reality when the beautiful young singer, Christine Daaé, suddenly disappears after her triumphant performance. An ever increasing pattern of fear and violence pervades the dim backstage areas and subterranean passages of the glorious Opera House as the phantom threatens to strike once more.

## THE RED BADGE OF COURAGE
*Stephen Crane*

Young Henry Fleming had always dreamt of performing heroic deeds in battle. But the reality, as a raw recruit in the American Civil War, is a mental and physical torment. And as Henry fights his inner battles with fear, self-doubt, trauma and vainglory throughout his first harrowing action, he has no idea whether war will make him a coward, a hero – or a man.

## THE RIME OF THE ANCIENT MARINER AND OTHER CLASSIC STORIES IN VERSE
*Edited by Robin Waterfield*

Mysterious, mythic, fabulous – this diverse collection is a wonderful introduction to the world of narrative verse. From the much-loved 'The Lady of Shalott' and 'The Pied Piper of Hamelin' to the less familiar 'The Raven' and 'Sohrab and Rustum', this is an anthology that will delight and surprise for years.

## THE SEA-WOLF
*Jack London*

When fate lands Humphrey Van Weyden on board
the Ghost, a sealing schooner bound for Japan,
little does he know of the weeks of brutality which
lie ahead. Captain Wolf Larsen is feared and
despised by all on board, and only the chance
arrival of Maud Brewster spurs Van Weyden into
action in a desperate attempt to free them both
from the terrifying power of the Sea-Wolf.

## SINDBAD THE SAILOR AND OTHER TALES FROM THE ARABIAN NIGHTS
*Retold by N. J. Dawood*

Sindbad, shipwrecked on exotic shores inhabited
by mythical beasts and flying men; the amazing
adventures of the Barber of Baghdad's six brothers;
how Ali Baba outwitted the forty thieves . . . The
daily entertainment of everyday people over a
thousand years ago, these Arabian, Indian and
Persian tales are full of magic and excitement.

PUFFIN CLASSICS

## THE TALE OF TROY
*Roger Lancelyn Green*

Freshly and excitingly written, this is the story of
Helen and the judgement of Paris; of the gathering
of the heroes and the siege of Troy; of Achilles
with his vulnerable heel, reared by the Centaur on
wild honey and the marrow of lions; of Odysseus,
the last of the Heroes, his plan for the Wooden
Horse and his many adventures on his long
journey home to Greece.

## TWENTY THOUSAND LEAGUES UNDER THE SEA
*Jules Verne*

A mission to rid the seas of a monster becomes a
nightmare for Professor Aronnax, Conseil and
harpooner Ned Land when they become prisoners
of the 'monster' itself – a spectacular submarine
ship commanded by Captain Nemo. But the
marvels of their underwater journey soon distract
them from their worries – the Professor, at least,
wouldn't have missed this voyage for the world!